"Your Janie?" His mother arched a brow.

"You know what I mean, Ma." He began to squirm under her sudden scrutiny. "Ah, not you, too! First that Kane fella tells Janie I have designs on her, then she accuses me of soundin' jealous, and now I'm gettin' the *look* from my own ma." He crossed his arms and glared at her. "It isn't like that between me and Janie."

"Mmm." His mother lifted her cup, blew delicately against the steam again, and took a dainty sip.

"It isn't! And you know it. It never has been."

"You'd know that better than I." She lifted the corner of her apron and gently tapped her lips. "If I can give you a woman's perspective, son, hearing compliments and sweet words whispered into her ear and feeling cherished and admired, counts a lot with a girl."

"Janie doesn't need all that silly stuff. She knows she's admired. Everybody admires her, or else why would she be elected sheriff?"

Isaac saw his mother come just short of rolling her eyes. As if she thought he was some dimwit. Her words confirmed it.

"For a smart boy, you're really. . .*really* not so smart. I've been trying to explain to you that Kane Braxton is telling Janie what she needs to hear. That she's lovely and cherished and adored. And why shouldn't he tell her that? It's the truth. And it makes her happy." She looked at Isaac sternly. "And who are you to say the man doesn't mean it? If you think Janie's so fine, why wouldn't he think so?"

"Okay! So you made your point." Isaac scowled. "But what if I'm right and he *is* just danglin' her along for his own pleasure, and he *does* break her heart?"

RACHEL DRUTEN is a native Californian. She is an artist as well as an author, wife, mother, and grandmother. Much of her time is devoted to overseeing a nonprofit, on-site after-school program in the arts for disadvantaged children, K through 5.

Books by Rachel Druten

HEARTSONG PRESENTS

Out of
the Ashes

Rachel Druten

Heartsong Presents

Dedicated to my husband, Charles.

Once again I acknowledge my quadrumvirate of editors, dear friends: Dianna Crawford, Sheila Herron, Barbara Wilder, and my husband, Charles, who is always willing to wield his red pencil; and, gratefully, my editors, JoAnne Simmons and Debra Peterson, who always help make my books better.

A note from the Author:
I love to hear from my readers! You may correspond with me by writing:

Rachel Druten
Author Relations
PO Box 721
Uhrichsville, OH 44683

ISBN 978-1-60260-303-5

OUT OF THE ASHES

All scripture quotations are taken from the King James Version of the Bible.

All of the characters and events in this book are fictitious. Any resemblance to actual persons, living or dead, or to actual events is purely coincidental.

Our mission is to publish and distribute inspirational products offering exceptional value and biblical encouragement to the masses.

PRINTED IN THE U.S.A.

one

"That Jackie Lee is one fine woman," mumbled a deep male voice behind Sheriff Jane McKee.

Standing in front of Whispering Bluff Post Office and Telephone Company, Jane was intent on watching her pretty older friend float across Main Street, a full-blown yellow rose in the whirl of her ruffled wool shawl.

Jane smiled at the man behind her. "Why, Big Jim Houston, you're blushing."

The handsome middle-aged farmer, whose tanned cheeks had turned crimson, secured the reins of his white stallion over the hitching rail as if he hadn't heard.

Big Jim was a legend in Whispering Bluff. Devout, generous, a pillar of the community, who owned the largest, most successful wheat farm in three counties. He had eschewed marriage in favor of raising his dead brother's four orphaned children. But Jane suspected his single status had as much to do with a secret passion for the winsome Jackie Lee. In a moment of youthful impetuosity, she'd been swept off her feet by the flashy charm of Jake August. To her ultimate regret.

Big Jim, obviously embarrassed at being caught dead to rights in his not-so-silent musing, put his silver-toed boot onto the boardwalk with a "Harrumph" and strode into Thompson's General Store without looking back.

Anyway, by now Jackie Lee had disappeared into Mavis Dodd's Couture and Chapeaux.

Jane could never remember seeing Jackie Lee so happy. It was about time. No one had suffered more all these years than

Jackie Lee, and as far as Jane was concerned, no one deserved it less.

But all that had changed. Isaac was coming home!

Jane was still smiling when she pushed open the post office door. "Morning, ladies. Anything for me, Henrietta?" she asked the sour-faced postmistress.

Maybe Isaac had written Jane a letter, too, although she could count on one hand those she'd received in the last four years. It was Jackie Lee who had kept Jane apprised of his whereabouts and what he was up to.

Even so, Jane knew that she and Isaac were soul mates and always would be, no matter where the wind blew him. They and Becca Hostetler—soon *Doctor* Becca—had made a vow the first day of grammar school and sealed it with a pinprick and exchange of blood. They'd been six years old, some eighteen years ago.

Henrietta Pryce, the postmistress, was in a huddle at the counter with Lilly Johnson, the mousy-haired, city hall secretary, and husky Naomi Pool, whose daddy owned the feedstore. Since Jackie Lee had just left, Jane figured she knew their topic. It was dangerous to be the first to leave when Henrietta was holding court, especially if one's name happened to be Jackie Lee.

"As a matter of fact I do have some mail for you. . .*Sheriff.*" Henrietta still lifted her brow at Jane's title, even though she'd had it nearly two years. She pulled a thin package from under the counter. "Your patterns from Butterick came, and a letter. . . Same address as hers." She rolled her eyes as she pushed the two pieces of mail across the high counter.

"Hers?" Jane knew very well who the busybody meant but wasn't about to let the middle-aged spinster get away with that kind of disrespect.

The postmistress looked down her narrow nose through beady black eyes. "The saloonkeeper's wife."

"Widow! Or hadn't you heard? Even though it's been over two months since Jake August died." Jane glared up at the skinny, apron-clad woman behind the counter, feeling venom quite against her usual sunny nature. Henrietta Pryce was the one person in town who tried the sheriff's good temper beyond all measure.

Jane turned to the two women standing next to her at the counter: Lilly, with that supercilious smirk, and Naomi, strong as an ox with a disposition as plodding.

Their meanness made her weary and less charitable than she wanted to be.

"I didn't see any of you at the funeral, either. It might have been a benevolent thing to do even if you didn't approve of that sinful old husband of hers."

"She chose him," Henrietta muttered, getting back to her sorting.

"Yes, she was just as fooled as some others in this town," Jane said.

"How would you know? You weren't even born," Henrietta mumbled.

It was rumored that Henrietta had also had her eye on Jake August in those days. Which may have accounted for some of her animosity.

Husky-voiced Naomi blustered, "I'd have kicked him out."

You'd have the muscle for it, Jane thought, eyeing the stocky woman. What she said was, "By the time Jackie Lee found out the man's true character it was too late; Isaac was on the way. Everybody knew, by then, that Jake had spent all her inheritance on that saloon, and she had no money of her own and a baby on the way. She had no choice but to stay with him."

"Well, he's dead now," Lilly said in her high, whispery voice.

"Yes, he's dead," Jane said, "leaving poor Jackie Lee up to her pretty neck in debt and only that den of iniquity to support her."

Jane had started the day really bright and happy, made even more so by Jackie Lee's good news, but now all this talk had really gotten her down in the dumps. It wouldn't last, she knew that, but the sooner she left this depressing company the better.

Still, she couldn't resist one last word. At the door she turned and faced the tittle-tattle troika. "Jackie Lee is one of the kindest people I've ever known. I've never heard her say one disparaging word about anybody. It's about time some of the God-fearing folk in this community took a page from her book."

At that moment Hazel Pryce, Henrietta's older sister, a near carbon copy but an inch shorter, poked her head through the door of the telephone office. "What's going on?"

"Ask these charitable Christian ladies. I'm sure they can give you an earful," Jane said, pushing through the post office door.

She was in such a hurry to read Isaac's letter that she paid little heed crossing Main and almost got run down by Eric Apple's buckboard—worthy of a warning from the sheriff, had she herself not been the sheriff.

"Sorry, Eric," she called, giving a chagrined wave as she reached the other side, stepped up onto the boardwalk, and hurried into her office.

"I'm back," she called to her deputy, Spike Terrell, who was mopping out the four cells for lack of anything better to do. "Anything on the ticker tape about the rustlers in Dodd County?"

"Quiet as usual," Spike intoned, continuing his tuneless humming in rhythm with the sloshing mop. Spike was a gravelly-voiced, lumbering bear of a man with a belly that reflected his hearty appetite.

Jane threw the packet of Butterick patterns on the desk, tearing open the letter as she plopped down into the leather chair. The same desk and chair her papa had occupied before he had suddenly died almost two years ago and Jane had been elected sheriff in his place—fitting, the townsfolk thought, since she'd done everything but wear the badge for her loving but indolent papa during his lifetime.

The old chair squeaked as she leaned back. She was tempted to cross her booted feet on the large, scarred desktop as her daddy had, but it was not an image she cared to perpetuate.

Besides, being sheriff made her no less a lady—even if she was the best shot in the county.

She felt a flutter of anticipation as she unfolded the letter.

Dear Sheriff Mighty Mite,

Well, stoke up the fire, I'm heading home. Already I'm salivating for those scones slathered with your famous lemon curd and a platter of your chocolate cookies all to myself.

That said, I hope I don't need to get arrested to warrant (got that, heh, heh, warrant) one of those good meals of yours that I've been dreaming about these last four years.

Imagine, Sheriff Jane. Little Sheriff Jane. I'm still having trouble putting a handle on it, even though I know you were your papa's right hand (and his left, and sometimes his two feet—now don't be offended, honey; I loved the man. You know that. A better heart never beat).

Will I recognize you? Or have you grown a foot taller? Are your curls still the color of ripe wheat? Your eyes cornflower blue? Have they crossed since I last saw you doing all that staring into the scope of that rifle of yours in the line of duty? Have you developed big muscles tossing all those drunks in the clink?

Ma says you're even prettier than ever. I say pretty is as pretty does. I can still remember those matted curls and your tiny fists pumping when you and I and Becca were defending Peter, fresh off the orphan train, against the Singletons when we were kids.

What ever happened to that clan of misfits?

Looking forward to seeing Becca and Peter, too. Ma says their marriage was made in heaven. I suppose Peter's running her daddy's farm by now. That worked out all the way around. Her daddy was looking to retire even before I left. And Becca graduating from doctor school—would you believe it? Dr. Becca. I suppose she'll be helping out Doc Warner. How old is he now? Near eighty, I reckon. He can use the help for sure. But who would have thought it would be our Becca?

Ma says I won't recognize the old town. Just as well; aside from you and Becca and Peter, I don't harbor many happy memories there.

That last beating from Pa laid me low for weeks. Can't say I was all that sorry when he kicked me out. Except, of course, leaving Ma in his talons. Even at that, I would have stayed, but she wouldn't let me.

I always regretted that you and I didn't get a chance to say good-bye, but Pa'd made up his mind and wasn't about to let the grass grow. Piled me in that first boxcar out of WB.

Bumpy ride.

But that's in the past, and so is he. Thank the good Lord!

Anyway, with him gone, the bad penny returns. I expect I'll stay a bit, help Ma get back on her feet, and then move on. Footloose and fancy-free seems to suit me.

Have some music business to wrap up here, but should be on my way by next week.

Gosh. This letter is long enough to make up for all the ones I didn't write all these years. Hope it gets there before I do.

Your wandering minstrel man,

Isaac

Her wandering minstrel man?

Was he still, after four years and as many letters? After all that time living the big-city life, all that he'd seen and experienced?

Would he still be her soul mate?

Or would he think her too "small town," too "country"?

two

Jane unhooked the receiver from the telephone mounted on the wall of the sheriff's office and waited for the nasal-voiced telephone operator to come on the line. "Hazel, will you please get me Becca?"

"Becca who?" was the prim reply.

Obviously the woman was still piqued over Jane's performance in the post office.

How many Beccas are there in this town of five hundred?

Jane took a deep, calming breath and said with supreme politeness, "Would you mind ringing Rebecca Wilcox Hostetler Chaloupek for me?"

"Oh, that Becca. Hold on."

Hazel made the connection, and after a click Becca's voice came on the line.

"Hello."

"Becca, it's Jane."

"I was about to call you. I'm picking up a couple of dresses Mavis altered, and I was hoping you'd have time for a visit?"

"Always! But wait till you hear the news." Jane could visualize her tall, dark-haired friend leaning against the wood-paneled wall of the entry in the Hostetler farmhouse, the receiver to her ear. "Isaac's coming home."

"Fantastic!" Becca exclaimed. "When?"

"I expect early next week."

"Oh, no. I'm leaving for school day after tomorrow. I won't see him till I get back in September."

"That's right. He'll be so disappointed."

"No more so than I. Save the details. I'm on my way."

Jane's desk faced the large office window fronting Main Street. It gave her a view to the corner of First and then east

11

up past the feedstore. The location was real helpful Saturday nights when all she need do was lean out the door to get full sight of the saloon on the other side of the block. Although, since old Jake August had died and Jackie Lee took over, there weren't as many problems at that end of the street.

Absently she played with Isaac's letter as she stared out the window.

It was no secret that had Jackie Lee known her husband would sell her daddy's farm out from under him—to buy a saloon, of all things—the marriage would never have happened. Her papa was on his deathbed when Jake made him sign the papers. It was clear to Jackie Lee then, and the rest of the town, that the saloon had been Jake's goal from the beginning.

If only Jackie Lee had chosen her first beau, Big Jim Houston, instead of being felled by that false love. Then her papa would have had the best of care in his last days, and Jackie Lee would have lived happily ever after.

But what was done, was done!

Jane knew the old flame still burned in Big Jim. She'd seen that today in front of the post office. But if there were any embers still smoldering in Jackie Lee's heart, feelings of unworthiness and pride had long since damped them down deep. And it appeared that's the way it would stay.

But one good thing had come out of the union between Jackie Lee and Jake August, and that was Isaac.

Sad to say, not everybody in town had valued Isaac the way she and Becca and Peter had.

"The apple doesn't fall far from the tree," Henrietta Pryce had been fond of saying, in her most disdainful way.

Jane glanced at the telephone. She wondered what folks were saying about Isaac now. For surely the party lines were buzzing, thanks to Hazel—who always made it her business to listen in.

Would the people of Whispering Bluff give dear Isaac a chance? Or would they, as Henrietta did, paint him with the same dark brush as his no-account father?

Jane rose and moved nervously about her office.

She was eager to see Isaac. So eager that the mere thought of him made her fairly quiver with excitement.

She plopped down on the sofa and plumped one of the burgundy velour pillows.

Jane had made the sheriff's office akin to a parlor, hoping the atmosphere might calm the clients—she shied away from calling them criminals—and inspire behavior more in keeping with the wingback chairs and settee, the tranquil scenes in the paintings, and the flowers on her desk. And the soft classical music she sometimes played in the Victrola.

Still, she knew no one had been fooled into thinking she was weak. She did her duty when called upon. Many a Saturday night, when Jake August was still alive, she'd filled the cells with his drunken cronies. And she'd even shot and killed a gunman. Right out there in front of the bank on a Sunday afternoon. The leader of the River Gang!

She shuddered, and prayed she'd never have to draw her revolver on another man as long as she lived.

So much had happened in the years since Isaac had gone. And even though she felt like the same girl as always, she knew she must have changed and wondered, again, how he would view her.

≈

With nothing much else to talk about other than crops and the weather, Isaac's impending arrival occupied much of the conversation in the small town the following week.

Just as Jane had most feared, people took sides about his character, even some of the good folks in Good Shepherd Community Church. Pastor Pike, who'd never met Isaac himself, even preached a sermon on the subject. Without mentioning any names, of course.

He was as eloquent as Jane had ever heard him, quoting Psalm 140: "Deliver me, O Lord, from the evil man. . . continually are they gathered together. . . . They have sharpened their tongues like a serpent; adders' poison is under their lips. . . .

Keep me, O Lord, from the hands of the wicked."

He didn't paint a pretty picture of the transgressors. But still some tongues continued to wag.

Meanwhile, Jackie Lee was sprucing up the saloon.

The same bold SALOON sign hung over the door, but inside the place was being transformed. So much so that the town's most notorious drunk, Otis Dengle, complained to Spike Terrell when the deputy dragged the scrawny derelict into the jail that Saturday night. Said it hardly looked like a decent bar anymore with all its fancy frills.

He lifted his rheumy eyes. "A decent drunk don't know where ta look no more," he slurred. "An' that purty pale green on the walls, it's anough ta make a man puke. Next thing, she'll be a paintin' the spittoons pink."

"No doubt," Jane murmured as Spike hauled Otis through her office. "But it's the only watering hole in town. So, I guess you and the boys'll just have to put up with it."

Wednesday, two days before Isaac was to arrive, Jackie Lee's pretty little blond barmaid burst into Jane's office.

Jane hopped up from her desk and ran to the frantic young woman. "Christa, what's the matter?"

"Oh, Sheriff, you've got to come quick. Miss Jackie Lee fell off the ladder and hurt her ankle. She said to fetch you."

"How did it happen?"

"She's redecorating the saloon, you know," Christa explained as the two hurried out of the office. "She was hanging curtains on the front window, and she reached too far over, and down she went."

And that was how Jane found herself taking Jackie Lee's place at the train station that Friday, two days later, to meet the train carrying Isaac back to Whispering Bluff.

three

It was just past noon on a crisp, clear April day. A brief rain the night before had stirred up the fresh scent of sprouting buffalo grass along the track and washed away all but a few of the last dirty patches of snow clinging to the north-side slats of the rickety old station.

From the east Jane heard the distant blast of the train's whistle. There it came, like a tiny ant on the horizon, moving faster and faster along the parallel silver ribbons of track, growing larger and larger, until she was engulfed in thick, swirling smoke. She closed her eyes, covering her face with one white-gloved hand as she clutched her small flowered hat with the other. The brakes squealed, metal ground against metal, sparking the silver wheels as the locomotive rolled to a stop alongside the platform.

The Pullman doors clanged open. The conductor shouted, "Whispering Bluff!", lowered the steps, jumped down, then reached up to help an elderly lady in a black feathered hat.

Jane bounced on the balls of her feet, looking from one passenger car to the next. She knew how disappointed Jackie Lee that she wasn't able to meet her beloved Isaac. Jane was sad for her sake, but not enough to diminish her own breathless anticipation.

A slender, dark-suited young man alighted from the lounge car.

Not Isaac, that was for sure! No suit or briefcase for Isaac. Anyway, the man was too tall!

"All aboard!" the conductor hollered.

But where is Isaac? He said he'd be on this train. Surely he would have let his mother know if things had changed.

The whistle blasted as the conductor hopped onto the step

and reached down to pull up the block.

Jane's heart plopped into her stomach. She took another look at the dark figure moving toward the baggage cart. A fancy fedora shielded his face.

Surely Isaac wouldn't be as dandified as that.

Just as she was about to check, she heard that still familiar voice behind her.

"Well, the mighty one is still a mite, I see."

She swung around, almost tripping on her own feet.

But this wasn't Isaac, this very tall young man, with very broad shoulders. A cowhand with his scuffed boots, weathered jeans, and Pendleton jacket. His face was hidden in the shadow of his black felt cowboy hat. But certainly, what she saw in no way resembled the bruised, spindly fellow who had left Whispering Bluff four years before.

It was the guitar case, swung over his shoulder, that gave Jane pause. . .and hope. And when he pushed back his hat revealing a mane of thick, curling cinnamon hair and those twinkling brown eyes and wide teasing grin, her heart leaped with certainty.

Catching her breath, she slapped her hands on her hips and smiled up at him. "I declare, Mr. Isaac, I didn't recognize you. Why, you've gotten so big and broad. . .and almost handsome."

"Well, I declare, Miss Mighty Mite," he said, impudently mirroring her stance, "you've gotten almost pretty."

He flung out his arms and she ran into them, locking her hands around his neck and throwing back her head in a paroxysm of joy. He circled the empty platform, her blue cape flying out like wings; Jane clinging to him, breathless, dizzy, and laughing.

Abruptly he stopped and plopped her down with a jolt. "Where's Ma?"

"Don't you worry," Jane said, gaining her balance and straightening her hat. "Your mama's going to be just fine."

"Goin' to be?" A worried frown creased his bronzed, lightly freckled face.

"She had a fall a couple of days ago and sprained her ankle. That's why she sent me with the buggy. . .to carry you home in style."

"Sounds like Ma, makin' things nice in the worst of times."

"I think she'd say your homecoming was the best of times," Jane asserted.

Isaac pulled his hat low, shadowing his eyes, but she could still see his mouth was set in a hard line.

"Don't you dare feel guilty for staying away, Isaac. As long as your papa was alive you had no choice."

"Didn't I?"

"No, you didn't. He was a bad man. Your mama wanted you safe from his cruelty. It was better the way it was. She told me that more than once. Even though she missed you with all her heart, she knew you were better off where you were."

Jane took both Isaac's hands in hers, forcing him to look at her. "In my professional opinion, Jackie Lee was safer, too."

Isaac looked down at her in silence, then smiled. "In your professional opinion. Well, that beats all."

"Don't make fun of me, Isaac August." Jane dropped his hands and thrust out her chin.

"Sorry, Sheriff. It's just a new wrinkle I have to get used to. Give me time. I'll catch on." He grinned, touching the brim of his hat. "And do my best to stay honest so I don't get in trouble with the law—unless I've got a hankerin' for a good meal. Are the crooks still getting the best vittles in town, thanks to your *culinary* skills?"

"As I recall, you'd help me whip up those vittles from time to time when Papa was sheriff."

"Which stood me in good stead in my various incarnations these last four years—among them fry cook in a New York eatery." He shook his head. "Another life, another time."

"Well, you're home now, and I hope to stay, despite what you said in your letter about being footloose and fancy-free. It's good to put down roots."

"It depends on how hospitable the soil," he said, frowning.

"With your papa gone, things'll be different, I promise."

"We'll see." Isaac shrugged. "Hey," he said suddenly. "Enough of this chitchat. Not that I haven't enjoyed it." He flashed her a smile. "But it's time I saw my mama."

He reached down and grabbed the smallest of the three bags and thrust it into Jane's hand. "Make yourself useful, Miss Janie." He gave her an affectionate swat.

"You forget whom you're dealing with, young man," she said archly, catching her balance. "The sheriff of Whispering Bluff is entitled to a certain degree of respect, after all."

"Yeah, yeah." Grinning, he adjusted the guitar strap on his shoulder, hefted the other two bags, and followed her toward the rickety steps at the end of the platform. "Where do you hide your six-shooter when you're not wearin' that voluminous cape, Miss Sheriff?" he asked, allowing his bold gaze to skim playfully over her.

"Don't be fresh with me, young man, or you'll find out why I'm the best shot in three counties."

"Those stairs don't look any safer now than they did four years ago." He elbowed her aside and bounded down the shaky steps. Before her foot hit the first riser he had dropped his satchels, turned, and in one swoop, swung her into the waiting buggy as if she were no heavier than a bag of goose down.

So much for respect!

Tossing in the luggage, he hopped up into the driver's seat.

"I recognize the buggy, but not the mare," he said, snapping the reins. "I expect a lot of things have changed since I left." He looked over at her. "But you haven't changed, Janie, not really. If anything you've gotten prettier. Sweeter remains to be seen. . .but clearly as feisty. I'm surprised some Whisperin' Bluff swain hasn't swept you up by now."

"Not much luck in that department."

"Too hard to please?"

"Maybe I just set my sights too high." She sighed.

"Never!" He glanced at her, his lips twitching. "What kind of sorry group of sissified dudes can't appreciate a hardfisted, flint-eyed, sharpshootin', curly-haired little sheriff? And they call themselves cowboys!"

Jane's shoulders slumped. "Maybe that's the problem."

"What?"

"Hard fists, flinty eyes, sharpshooting. . .sheriff."

"You mean those poky cowpokes feel intimidated?"

"Do you suppose?" She gave him an oblique glance. "I'm not saying all of them, of course."

He reached over and gave her hand a brotherly pat. "All they need is to be educated to your softer side. I am going to make that my goal, before movin' on."

"Then I reckon you'll be staying a piece." Jane smiled. "I've come to think maybe I'm not the marrying kind. I've been burned enough times not to cotton to carrying the torch again, leastways, not in the foreseeable future. Besides, I'm quite content with my life the way it is. I have my job, my friends"—she gave him a fond smile—"and my faith. That's enough for now. Thank you for your concern, Isaac, but no need."

four

Isaac shook his head. Not the marrying kind? Who did she think she was fooling? This was old Isaac she was talking to.

What had happened to make her change her tune? Although he didn't believe it for a minute.

Growing up all she could talk about was having a home and a passel of young'uns to sew and cook for.

He flicked the reins, urging the mare into a trot. Out of the corner of his eye he observed his little friend tucked into the seat beside him, wisps of blond curls blowing about her rosy cheeks as she chattered on about the local happenings—not all that earthshaking in Whispering Bluff—but to her credit, she managed to make them amusing.

He'd expected her to change, and she had. Her curls were more golden, her eyes a deeper blue. When he'd left she was a perky girl; now she was a woman.

But when she'd tilted her head and given him that look at the station—and opened her smart mouth—the years fell away.

"Becca and Peter...the Aubreys..."

What had she said? He'd missed it in his musings.

"I'm eager for you to meet them. He's the schoolmaster. A playwright and a poet like you. You'll like each other."

For a moment her gaze turned outward toward the plains, pensive, her tiny gloved hands clasped tightly in her lap. He felt he was observing a quiet, secret part of her that wasn't as brave and carefree as the happy facade she was so determined to present to the outside world.

In four years she'd had her disappointments, too; her dreams dashed...her heart broken. Maybe more than once from what his ma had written.

He'd like to get his hands on the cads who'd broken it. Of all the people who didn't deserve to be hurt it was sweet little Jane, who'd never hurt a soul.

Except to save another.

He couldn't believe she'd actually shot and killed a man.

On the other hand, why was he so surprised? That had always been a part of her nature, too: Jane, the sharpshooter, the champion of justice and truth, the upholder of law and order. He knew how tough she could be. She'd shown her courage from the time they were children and she'd stood up to those Singleton bullies.

Oh yes! He'd seen that side of her, many times. In fact, he'd seen just about every side of her there was to see.

But now, as he gazed over at her, he was struck again by her wistfulness, the hint of sadness.

Well, by gum, he was going to make things right for her before he moved on. It was the least he could do, if for no other reason than her kindness to his ma. Being her friend all these years when she'd had so few.

No siree, Janie's smile should never have a shadow. And as long as he was here he'd see it never did.

As he looked out over the sun-drenched fields plowed for spring planting, he smelled the rich loam of freshly turned earth. He'd missed it. His gaze traveled south to the copse of cottonwoods that shaded Rikum's Pond. Good memories. And ahead to the schoolhouse perched on its solitary knoll like a miniature white toy—not so good. His feelings for Whispering Bluff were decidedly mixed.

He had missed his mother, of course, and Becca, and Peter, but most of all he had missed Jane, his soul mate, his confidante, his closest friend.

What he hadn't missed was a father who abused him and the townsfolk who, with few exceptions, saw him only as the saloonkeeper's son.

No, there had been little reason for him to hurry back to Whispering Bluff except for Ma. . .and Jane.

"I must say, Isaac," Jane said, bringing him back to the present, "you were hardly a font of information the last few years."

"I sent you Christmas cards."

"Card. Singular."

"That's all?"

She nodded.

"I could have sworn—"

"And four letters. The last being three weeks ago."

"You're sure?"

"I can prove it!"

"You saved 'em?" He looked over at her with a grin. "I'm touched. Truth is, I didn't have much to write about the first couple years. Just drifted." He smiled ruefully. "If I'd written it would probably been on an old paper bag with a piece of charcoal from a campfire along the tracks. I couldn't have sent it anyway. Couldn't afford beans, let alone postage."

"I had no idea." Jane looked so distressed he quickly reassured her.

"Made a lot of friends, though. Hoboes like me, who shared what vittles they had. And songs." He glanced at the guitar case lying on the seat behind him. "I reckon my old guitar was my best buddy in those days. Many's the night I held it in my arms like a mama cradles her baby." He snapped the reins. "It wouldn't have been there come mornin' if I hadn't had a tight grip. Yep, I picked up music during those years I'd have never discovered otherwise: railroad songs, folk songs, cowboy songs. That's how hoboes keep themselves entertained when they aren't all liquored up. . .and sometimes when they are."

"I would have thought your papa would have been a lesson in that regard," she murmured.

"Don't worry, Janie; I don't touch the stuff."

She looked relieved and rested her head against his shoulder. "Jackie Lee never told me how hard it was for you."

"You think I told her? She had enough worries without me adding to 'em."

"You could have written me for money; you know that."
Jane straightened. "A loan to get you back on your feet. You
would have done it for me."

"How do you know? You never put me to the test." He
smiled. "I would be whoppin' mad if you didn't ask. But a
man's different. He's got to prove himself." Then he laughed,
pumping his fist. "And I'm a better man for it."

"That remains to be seen," Jane said, tilting her pointy chin
and looking at him with such genuine warmth that, for the
moment at least, he was glad to be back.

He drove on a piece. "So you kept my letters, did you? All
tied up in pink ribbon?"

"More like leftover string from the feed bag."

"But you kept 'em."

"It was all I had of you. Who knew if you'd ever come back?
Although I always thought you would someday."

"Well, that day has come, Miss Janie. Here I am, the bad
penny, the wandering minstrel man."

"Yes, here you are." Jane observed him quietly for a moment.
"You left a boy; you came home a man!" She sighed. "Until
you opened your mouth."

He shook his head. "Janie, Janie."

"I did love your letters, though. . .the *few* that I got—"

"Keep rubbin' it in."

"They were quite wonderful. That's why I kept them. They
were funny and full of such colorful stories I sometimes
doubted your veracity."

"With good reason. Often the truth was not pretty."

"They sounded so much like you," Jane continued. "And I
love the songs you wrote. I think you should do something
with them, Isaac."

"That's why I ended up in New York."

"I thought you said you were a cook."

"That was until Buffalo Bill showed up in Chicago with his
show and I found out that if you can play a guitar and wear
boots and a cowboy hat, you're a cowboy singer. Especially in

New York. From then on I was able to sing for my supper."

By now they could see the steeple atop Good Shepherd Community Church peeking over the rise.

"Just before I left, a man wanted to show some of my songs to a music publisher," Isaac said absently.

Jane bounced up in her seat. "Why, Isaac, that's terrific."

"It's happened before and nothin' came of it." He shrugged. "And now with me gone. . ."

"That's a very bad attitude," Jane admonished. "You just never know. I certainly hope you told him where you could be reached."

He grinned. "Of course I did. Ya think I'm dim?"

"Don't ask." Jane threw him a teasing smile.

"I told you. I'm a new man," he retorted, rounding the curve from Mulberry Street onto First.

They had passed the church and the parsonage, but just as they were about to turn left onto Main, Isaac pulled to the side of the road, suddenly apprehensive.

Jane glanced up. "Why are you stopping? Don't tell me you're nervous about seeing your mama?"

He smiled ruefully. "Maybe a little." He held the reins loosely between his knees and turned to look at her. "Has she changed much?" He frowned. "I mean. . .does she look a lot older? I guess I'm kinda worried about what I'm gonna find."

Jane patted his arm. "If anything, your mama's prettier than ever—now that your papa's gone! Not that I mean any disrespect for the dead, but you know. . ." She went on. "Yes indeed, your coming home has given her new purpose, that's for sure. Mrs. Meade says your mama's like she was when they were girls. And you won't believe the changes she's made in the saloon. You may have trouble recognizing it—aside from the sign, of course. She's painted it inside and out and. . .well, you'll see."

"That's got to be a sight."

"And she serves food now, too," Jane said.

"Pa must be turning over in his grave," Isaac whooped.

"Not fancy food, just simple fare, but very nourishing. In fact, I gave her my recipe for three-bean soup. And she has a standing order with Trudy for whole grain bread."

"Well that beats all. So, what was the reaction of the fine ladies of Good Shepherd Community Church?"

Jane rolled her eyes.

"I can just imagine," Isaac said, more serious now.

"However, Pastor Pike remains unfazed," Jane assured him. "In fact, last Sunday he preached a very pointed sermon on how the Lord honored and blessed those who gave generously of their compassion, not mentioning any names of course, but everybody knew whom he was talking about. Then he looked directly at the congregation and quoted part of a verse from First Timothy, chapter six, challenging them not to be 'highminded, nor trust in uncertain riches, but in the living God, who giveth us richly all things to enjoy.' I thought it was a brilliant sermon, myself. As expected of course, there were several pouty faces. But everybody got the picture."

"Yes, indeed, Isaac, you're going to be real surprised at all the changes, and I reckon not at all displeased." Jane gave his arm another pat. "So drive on. You don't have a dot to worry about. Not so much as one tiny dot."

Isaac looked down at her sweet animated face and shrugged. "If you say so, Miss Mighty Mite." He flicked the reins and the mare obediently trotted forward. "If you say so."

She might be right, but Isaac's bruised heart told him otherwise. That's why, as the buggy rolled up the center of Main, he looked neither to the right nor to the left. He was not yet ready to suffer the contemptuous gazes of the good folks of Whispering Bluff.

five

Shortly before noon, less than a week after Isaac arrived, Jane spotted him across the street. He was coming out of the post office with two large packages.

Just the person she was looking to see.

She stuck her head out her office door. "Yoo-hoo, Isaac!" She waved.

Isaac crossed the street and hopped up onto the boardwalk. "Howdy, Mighty Mite."

"Those look important." She scanned the colorful labels. "More fabric?"

"For tablecloths." He grinned. "You'd think Ma was decorating a fancy New York eatery instead of a saloon. What's up?"

"It's Thursday."

"So?"

"You remember, Thursday's choir practice night."

"Still?" He looked down at her with bemusement. "I'm sure they scratched me off the rolls long ago."

"You'll have no trouble being reinstated. We need baritones who read music."

He laughed. Actually it was more of a snort. "If I showed up, they'd clear the room."

"That's ridiculous," Jane scoffed.

"Not so ridiculous. From what I understand, folks aren't fallin' all over themselves to welcome old Jake August's widow back into the fold. I doubt it'd be any better for his boy."

Jane would have liked to say it wasn't so, but to an extent, Isaac spoke the truth. Many were merciful in Good Shepherd Community Church, but some were also what Jane considered hypocrites—people who tolerated folks to their face and talked about them behind their backs.

In Jackie Lee's case it seemed particularly unfair. Everybody knew Jackie Lee's family had been among the original founders of Good Shepherd Community Church. But when she married Jake August, he'd had none of it, and even forbade her to attend on Sunday.

He wanted no goody-goody Christian competing for the devil in his soul.

Now, with the old reprobate dead, Jane was sadly disappointed that the community hadn't welcomed Jackie Lee back. Of course it didn't help that the poor widow was still operating the saloon. There was some prejudice about that. Although anybody with any sense knew that until she figured out a way to pay off her husband's debts, she had no choice, at least for now.

"In all fairness, though," Jane said mildly, "your mama doesn't give folks much of a chance to greet her. She and Christa and Maria sneak in after the service has begun, and they're out before the last hymn is finished."

"Would you want to wait around to be shunned?" Isaac frowned. "I've been here less than a week, and I've already gotten a taste of it."

Jane leaned against the doorjamb. "What happened?"

"I walked into the post office a few minutes ago to pick up Ma's packages, and those biddies at the counter suddenly fell silent as a wake. Wouldn't even look in my direction."

"Oh, pshaw. You can't judge everyone in Whispering Bluff by that little coterie of crones. Come on, Isaac," she wheedled. "You used to love the choir."

He still looked uncertain, but he was softening.

"John and Mary Aubrey are members. Mary's the accompanist."

"The schoolmaster and his wife?"

She nodded. "Mavis Dodd's a member."

"I noticed she'd opened Couture and Chapeaux. Pretty fancy name for dresses and hats." Isaac grinned.

"Adds a little class to the community, don't you think?" Jane remarked with an indulgent smile. "And Luke Thompson and his son—"

"Danny?" Isaac asked with surprise.

Jane nodded. "It takes him longer to catch on to things, for sure, but everyone's very patient with him. Being in the choir has given him a lot of confidence. He has a real talent for music. Once he learns a song he never forgets it. In fact, it turns out he has a fine voice. Pru told him when he sings a solo there's always more money in the collection plate. She says it joking, but I suspect there's a tad of truth, she calls on him so often. A full collection plate doesn't hurt, since that's what a pastor lives on. That and the missionary barrels. . .and in this case, the largesse of Big Jim Houston, although the Pikes don't know it," Jane confided. "More than once I've seen Big Jim reach into his wallet a second time and secretly add to the coffers when he doesn't think it's sufficient.

"He's in the choir, too. He'd be real nice to you." She smiled slyly. "I know for certain he still holds a warm spot in his heart for your mama. Though she's too proud"—*and too ashamed*, Jane added silently—"to even glance in his direction. Sad to say."

"I remember Ma tellin' me how he used to court her before Pa entered the picture." Isaac shook his head.

Neither spoke for a moment, considering what might have been.

Then Jane gazed up into Isaac's brown compassionate eyes and almost handsome face. "I reckon Jackie Lee wouldn't change a thing if it meant not having her precious son."

"I hope you're right," Isaac said, looking up the street toward the saloon. "Some called me Jake's bad seed."

"That sprouted into a strong tree," Jane assured him.

"Time will tell."

Jane took a deep breath. It was too bright a morning to be darkened any longer with recrimination and regrets. Besides, she still had not achieved her purpose.

"So, I expect you to escort me to choir practice this evening, Mr. August. I will be ready to receive you at fifteen minutes before the hour."

Isaac cocked his head. "Did I say that I was goin'? I didn't hear that."

"By implication."

"What implication?"

"The implication that I'll nag you until my last breath unless you do. Skedaddle now, your mama's waiting for her packages."

Before he could protest, Jane had whirled around and slipped through her office door, where she turned and pressed her nose against the glass and stuck out her tongue, just as she used to when they were children.

❧

So it was that Isaac showed up that evening to escort Jane to choir practice.

The door of Jane's little cottage flew open as he stepped up on the porch.

Uh-oh, he thought, seeing his little friend already wrapped in her ruffled cape and wearing a decidedly irritated expression.

"You're late!"

"Sorry."

"You knew choir practice started at seven. It's that now." She shut the door behind her and hurried down the steps ahead of him.

"I thought it was seven thirty," he fudged.

"If you'd thought it was seven thirty you would have arrived fifteen minutes later. It only takes five minutes to get to church," she groused, continuing to march ahead.

Then suddenly she stopped and waited for him to catch up. She looked up at him, her voice gentling. "You're reluctant, aren't you?"

He shrugged.

That put it mildly. He dreaded it. Especially after his little episode in the post office. The only reason he was going was to please her.

"I don't blame you." She took his arm and hurried on again, cutting kitty-corner across Main Street. "But I'm doing it for your own good. It'll be fine, trust me."

This wasn't the first time Jane had insisted he should attend choir. And more than once he had paid for it with a beating from his pa.

He shuddered. Not from fear—he'd outgrown that—but from loathing.

"You cold? You should have worn a heavier jacket."

"Not cold. Just rememberin' my pa and the beatings."

In all those years Jane was the only one in whom he could confide and be sure she would understand, and it would go no further. Amazing how it was still so.

He glanced down at her, the hood of her cape thrown back, her blond curls bouncing as she hurried up the church steps.

She paused at the top landing. "You had a lot of courage for a young boy, Isaac. You came to choir in spite of him."

"Stubborn is more like it." He shrugged. "If not sneaky. It gave me a kick to be able to put one over on him."

"Even when you didn't?"

"It was worth the risk." He grinned. "Remember how our Sunday school teacher, Becca's ma, made us memorize the Ten Commandments? She was big on honorin' your father and your mother."

"So you honored your mother." Jane pushed open the church door, dragging him after her. "And you remembered the Sabbath. . .and one or two of the others."

She grinned up at him and he tousled her curls, feeling better.

"I remember when Jacob Hostetler gave me my first guitar. It changed my life," he mused, following her through the narthex to a side hall that ran the length of the sanctuary.

They saw a light under the door to the choir room at the end and heard voices, warming up.

As they entered, the room fell silent.

Isaac felt the sweat collect under his arms as he stared at the two rows of solemn faces staring back at him.

A small, pretty woman with brown hair pulled into a neat

knot at her nape, turned soft, fawn-colored eyes on him and laid her baton on the music stand. She walked over smiling as she extended both hands.

"Isaac. Welcome. Jane's told me so much about you."

"This is Pru Pike, our esteemed choir director and wife of the pastor." Jane turned to Pru. "I'm so sorry we're late. There was a mix-up on time—"

"You mustn't apologize. I'm just so glad you're both here." She turned to the seated choir members. "Some of you already know Isaac, but for those who don't, I want you to welcome Jackie Lee August's son."

Well that was laying the cards on the table. Now we'll see what plays out.

To his surprise, the faces lit with smiles—some broader than others—and a murmuring of things like, "Welcome, Isaac," "Hello there," and "Good to see you," passed along the line.

While Jane hurried to the empty chair in the soprano section Pru said, "Jane tells me you're a baritone, Isaac. Is that right?"

He nodded.

"If you gentlemen will move down a seat, I'm going to put Isaac between John and Danny."

In the front row a lovely lass with a thick auburn corn braid crowning her head blinked coyly from beneath thick lashes, her pouty lips lifting in a beguiling smile.

This choir had possibilities after all.

From the piano a pretty, dark-haired woman smiled encouragement, as if she understood his hesitation.

Mary Aubrey.

With a bit of shuffling, another chair was fitted in.

As Isaac slid into his designated seat, he nodded at Big Jim Houston sitting on the other side of John Aubrey. He glanced in Jane's direction, but the auburn-haired girl's eager, smiling face blocked his view.

"Please turn to hymn 142, 'Jesus Shall Reign.' " Pru lifted her baton.

❧

Afterward, as Isaac and Jane walked together down the front steps of the little church, Jane asked, "So, how was it?"

He took a deep breath. "Good. It was good. Just like old times."

"You'll keep coming then."

"As long as I'm here."

"Everyone was nice, weren't they?"

"Uh-huh." He reached for her arm as she took the last step.

"Especially Betty Jean Gordon," Jane said. "She was *real* nice. She almost created a cyclone, the way she was batting those long dark eyelashes of hers. Near blew the pages out of my hymnal."

"She's too young."

Jane gave him a sidewise grin. "She's eighteen. That's marrying age in these parts."

"I prefer 'em old and seasoned." He grinned down at her.

"Very funny. Seasoned at least I'll believe, judging from what I've heard about those wild women in the East."

"I thought it was the West that was supposed to be wild."

"That's the men. The women are demure and sweet."

"Lady sheriffs, too?"

"The significant word being *lady*!" She yanked her arm away in mock exasperation. "Even when they're old."

Isaac laughed. "Don't worry. To me you'll always be young, Mighty Mite, and ever a lady." He dropped his arm around her shoulders and gave her a warm hug.

They continued on in companionable silence.

"I think it's nice the way Pru wants you to bring your guitar next time," Jane said.

"As if she had a choice. The way you touted my talent one would have thought I was Tom Mix, the singin' cowboy."

"Danny Thompson sure got excited." She looked up at him. "It was sweet of you to tell him you'd give him guitar lessons."

"It pleased his dad," Isaac observed.

"Luke Thompson's bringing that boy up alone, and it isn't

easy. That was really kind of you."

"He's lucky to have a dad who cares," Isaac murmured.

They turned the corner onto Main.

"Do you want to come in for some hot chocolate?" Jane asked.

"If you insist."

As they approached Jane's cottage, Isaac gave a contented sigh and looked up into the heavens. "Wow. The stars look close enough to grab." And then he paused. "What's that?"

"What's what? I don't see anything."

"Over there." He pointed northeast.

Jane raised her eyes.

A soft pale ball of light was just beginning to spill over the horizon like warm honey, out beyond where Mulberry Street intersected the road leading from town.

As they watched, it suddenly exploded into a splash of orange.

"A fire," Jane whispered, her heart pounding.

six

It was the schoolhouse. Burned to the ground. By the time the fire wagon and the volunteers had arrived, nothing remained but a few charred timbers smoldering in the darkness, the scorched stove, the flagpole, the hitching posts. . .and the outhouse.

There was conjecture around town the next day as to how it started, discussed thoroughly by the regulars who hung out at Cutter Molten's barbershop, and around the stove at Thompson's General Store, and in front of the post office. Folks generally agreed it was probably arson, and had a good idea who the arsonist might be.

The day before, Jane had been looking out her office window when Ludd Morgan rode into town heading for the post office where Big Jim Houston was having a conversation with Jacob Hostetler.

Uh-oh.

Where Ludd Morgan went, trouble followed.

She pinned on her badge and reached for her holster hanging on the hook behind the door.

Sprinting out of her office, she arrived at the post office just as the squat, bowlegged cattleman swung off his horse.

He wasn't much bigger than Jane, his skin cracked and leather-hard from the sun. A mat of coarse gray hair sprouted like dry weeds from the open collar of his faded blue shirt.

If you were to ask anybody in town the color of Ludd Morgan's eyes, they'd be at a loss. All anybody saw were slits beneath the broad brim of his sombrero, a red, bulbous nose, and a tight, mean mouth that looked to have been cut above his chin by a thin blade.

Tethering his horse to the hitching rail, he hopped up onto the boardwalk and headed straight for the two men.

He poked Big Jim's chest with a crusted fist. "Where da you come off building a fence along my property? That's free-range land!"

"Aw, Ludd, you know better than that," Big Jim drawled. "That was surveyed and sold off by the government months ago. I bought three sections, fair and square."

Most men would have taken offense at Ludd's physical affront, but Big Jim was slow to anger. He just pushed his cowboy hat back on his head and gave the little weasel a slow, conciliatory smile.

Which only seemed to fuel the rancher's anger. "I was there first. Why. . .why my pa come to these parts when there weren't nothin' but a bunch of thievin' Injuns. We paid for this land with our blood and years of toil and sweat. And you farmers think you can jest come in and take anything you want. Tain't fair. Tain't fair at all. I need that land to graze my cattle."

"It ain't like you were took by surprise," Big Jim replied mildly. "The signs for the land sale have been up for months all over town and in the post office. They still are. If it wasn't me that bought that parcel, it woulda been somebody else. Heck, why didn't you buy it yourself, if you needed it all that bad?"

"Where'm I gonna get that kinda cash?" the little man sputtered.

"From the bank," Jacob Hostetler said. "The same as Jim did." The distinguished-looking farmer standing tall beside Big Jim had been watching the bandy-legged little bantam with amused detachment.

Ludd wasn't ready to let up. "My herd's been grazin' that free range since we settled here. Without it, I'd have to sell off half my cattle. By rights, it belongs to me." Spittle sprayed with his venom. He was standing up to Big Jim now, belly to belly, his pugnacious chin thrust forward, barely as high as the big man's collarbone.

Big Jim looked disgusted, shook his head, and took a step back.

"Believe it or not, Ludd," Jacob interjected, "there isn't one set of rules for you and another set for the rest of us. It's time you got that straight and stopped whining."

Jane saw that Jacob Hostetler, a gentleman to the core, was at the end of his patience.

He crossed his arms and looked down at Ludd with barely concealed disdain. "If you want your free range, you'll have to take your cattle somewhere else."

"Ya'd like to run me out, wouldn't all ya, all ya sniveling clod busters!" Ludd's chin jutted out even further. "Well ya ain't gonna do it. Ya ain't!"

Jacob gave the little rancher a level look. "All I know is you're going to have to pay for your land just like everybody else. And I happen to know you can afford to."

It was hard to gauge Ludd Morgan's worth, he was such a seedy-looking character, but Jane knew he was as rich as anyone in the county. And when it came to money, or what he thought was owed him, Ludd Morgan did not cotton to being crossed. To make matters worse, a group of townsfolk had gathered at the ruckus and obviously harbored little sympathy for him.

"No puny fence is gonna keep my cattle from grazin' that land," Ludd spat.

Big Jim bent down and looked Ludd in the eye, his gaze unflinching. "You just try it!"

Ludd was bouncing up and down with fury. "You don't know who yer messin' with, Big Jim Houston."

"Oh, I think I do, Ludd." Big Jim's voice was all steel now.

But Ludd still wasn't backing down. The crowd had grown and now his pride was at stake. "You may think yer a big shot, but yer not! You don't own this town."

"I own what I paid for," Big Jim retorted through gritted teeth. If he'd been so inclined, he could have flattened the little rooster right then and there. But violence had never been the solution for Big Jim Houston.

Not so for Ludd Morgan, whose threatened pride and vicious temper was a volatile brew. Jane took a deep breath. She'd seen Ludd explode before, with less cause than this.

"Why don't you stop your bellyachin', Ludd?" came a voice from the crowd.

Ludd whirled around. "Who said that?"

"Good idea," chided a woman to his left, ducking behind her bearded husband.

"Go back where you belong," a man called from behind Jacob.

Ludd automatically reached toward his holster.

Deftly Jane stepped forward and put a conciliatory hand on his shoulder. "Now, Ludd, we don't need trouble." She looked over at Big Jim. "As for you, Big Jim, your hair looks a mite shaggy around the collar. Why don't you and Jacob mosey over to the barbershop and get Cutter to give you a trim?"

Big Jim looked at Jacob and laughed. "If you say so, Sheriff." The two turned and ambled back down the boardwalk toward the barber's pole sticking out on the other side of the feedstore.

Ludd tried to shrug away from Jane's confining hand. "Get yer paw off me, girl."

But Jane's grip remained firm, then softened suddenly as she slid her arm around his slight shoulders. She put her mouth close to his ear, and in a voice only he could hear, whispered, "I may be only a girl, Ludd, but I'm still sheriff, and I've got the hardware to prove it. Now you behave yourself or I'm gonna use it. You know I will." She gave him a hard look, then dropped her arm, allowing a more mild gaze to sweep the small crowd. "I'm sure you folks have other things to attend to."

Muttering under his breath, Ludd threw Jane a last venomous glare. The remaining folks stepped aside as he strode across the boardwalk, his boots making a resounding whack on the wooden planks. In what seemed a single motion he had loosed the reins from the hitching rail and swept up onto his mount. Viciously, he dug his spurs into his horse's flank.

As the animal shot forward, he shouted over his shoulder, "This whole town can go up in smoke as far as I'm concerned!"

Which was how the rumor started.

seven

Ludd must have gotten wind of the rumor, because he had the sense to stay clear of town. Jane patrolled, putting out small eruptions of blame before they burst into flame, reminding folks that no evidence pointed to Ludd Morgan. "A man is innocent until *proven* guilty." That was the law.

There'd be no lynch mob on her watch.

Two days after the fire, when the school board and the city council—one and the same—were still pondering what to do, Pastor Pike offered the fellowship hall of Good Shepherd Community Church. It was a far piece for some children, but a viable solution until a new schoolhouse could be built. John Aubrey immediately made a long-distance telephone call to Denver for enough school supplies to last until the end of the term.

Late that afternoon, as Jane stepped out of her office to go home for supper, up the street Cutter Molten turned the closed sign in the barbershop window and Rush Berry rattled by in his ice wagon. At that moment, a stranger on a gray stallion rounded the corner at Main and First and rode toward her. He sat tall in the saddle, managing his restless mount with easy control.

Everything about him bespoke wealth, from the top of his expensive dove-gray Stetson to the tip of his elaborately tooled boots set firmly in silver-studded stirrups. Beneath the folds of his stylish gray greatcoat, Jane spied an intricately carved saddle and equally crafted saddlebags resting on his stallion's muscled flanks. The great steed tossed its head, rearing slightly as he reined to a halt.

He tipped his hat revealing gilded curls above a patrician brow, an aquiline nose and sculpted cheek, a golden mustache brushing wide, sensuous lips.

Jane could not have imagined a more comely example of manhood.

Indeed, he was so handsome she had to glance away to catch her breath. And look again to be sure he was not a wishful figment of her willful imagination.

His gray eyes radiated a silver glint and genuine surprise as he lowered his gaze to the star pinned on the blouse of her workday denim uniform.

"*You* are the sheriff?"

Nothing under heaven could have prepared her for the infusion of warmth elicited by the sound of his rich Southern baritone.

She nodded, swallowed, struggling to find her voice, which, to her dismay, came out in a squeak she hardly recognized. "What can I do for you, sir?"

His wide, handsome smile, obviously conceived to put her at ease, had quite the opposite effect. Her throat tightened. Her palms grew moist.

"Perhaps you can direct me to a boardinghouse in town?"

"We've only one, sir." She gulped, struggling to pull herself together. "You passed it as you came in."

Steadying herself against the rail, she pointed back down Main. "Turn on First. Where it hits Mulberry Street, on the southwest corner, there's a sign, TRUDY ST. CYR'S BOARD AND ROOM. You can't miss it."

"It appears I did." His smile broadened. "But with your directions I'm sure I'll find it this time. Thank you. . .Miss Sheriff." He adjusted the brim of his hat.

Jane cleared her throat. "May I ask your name, sir?"

He relaxed back into his saddle. "Kane Braxton. And yours?"

"Jane McKee."

"*Sheriff* Jane McKee!"

She nodded.

"It's unusual to see a lady sheriff."

She wanted to say, *A lady sheriff who's the best shot in three counties,* but it was against her nature to boast. "Folks are forward-thinking here in Whispering Bluff."

"Clearly. But one so young. . .and so very lovely." His Southern accent, caressing each word, thickened with the compliment.

Jane wasn't used to such silken praise from the country boys in Whispering Bluff and was quite at a loss for a response. She looked down at her clasped hands, and up into his expectant smile. "Ah. . . Do you have business in Whispering Bluff, Mr. Braxton? Or. . .or are you just passing through?"

He looked down with barely veiled amusement and a teasing twinkle in his eyes. "Are you asking as sheriff, Miss McKee?"

"Should I be?" she responded, her voice suddenly sharp.

His too-knowing look slapped some sense into her, and the suspicion that he was toying with this innocent country girl, delighting in her discomfort.

As if he'd intuited her reaction he said, "To be honest, I'm not sure what my business is. It all depends. You might say I'm on a quest. I've spent the last year searchin' for a place that feels like home. Where I can buy land and set down roots." His tone had turned reflective and his eyes were looking into space, seeing dreams, almost as if he were talking to himself. As if Jane weren't standing there at all.

She watched him silently. He was somewhat older than she had first imagined, a worldly man, by the look of him. What had brought such a man to an out-of-the-way place like Whispering Bluff?

"It's a good place, Whispering Bluff," she said quietly. "Nice folks that help each other. Everything we need is here, as you can see." She inclined her head toward the comfortable, business-lined street behind her. "Various different shops and services. A bank, a church, a school. . .or we had one until two days ago."

"Was it the remains of the schoolhouse that I saw, riding into town?"

"If you rode the easterly route, past the foundry."

"It must have been some fire," he said.

Jane nodded. "The children will be meeting in the church until it can be rebuilt."

"It sounds like you have a real sense of community here."

"We do."

He was quiet then, thoughtful. Finally he said, "If the rest of the folks in this town are like you, I expect I'm going to like it here." He straightened. "Like it very much."

The crickets and the katydids had begun their clacking. The sky had darkened enough to see a few stars sprinkling the heavens.

Jane pushed back a recalcitrant curl.

She could feel his watching.

"Well. . .I won't keep you any longer." Kane Braxton lifted his hand to the brim of his hat in a two-finger salute. "I suspect we'll be seeing more of each other in the days to come, Sheriff Jane McKee. If I stay." He flicked the reins and wheeled his stallion around.

Jane watched as he cantered down Main in the direction that he'd come, then turned onto First, where he was hidden from her view by Norwood Bank on the corner.

Kane Braxton!

Even the name made her shiver.

Not that this Kane Braxton was her type, too old for one thing. He had to be at least eight or nine years older than she was, and way too fancy.

She chuckled to herself. But it did show that this girl still had red blood running through her veins.

"What are you laughin' about, Miss Mighty Mite?"

Jane whirled around. "Myself, Minstrel Man."

"That was a fancy-looking dude."

"Wasn't he!"

"Doesn't look much like the Whispering Bluff type."

Jane shook her head. "You're such an expert. What is our type? Dim-witted and countrified?"

Not that it wasn't her thought, too, but hearing it come out of Isaac's smart mouth made the Whispering Bluff folks all sound so. . .so provincial. Now and then he had this know-it-all quality that really irritated her. As if his vast experience in the big city had somehow given him special insight.

"I didn't say dim-witted." He tickled her in the ribs.

She shrugged him away. "No. But that was your implication."

"If the shoe fits." He laughed.

"For your information, he likes it here," she sniffed. "Says he might just stay a piece, try Whispering Bluff on for size. See if the shoe fits, as you so aptly put it." She started walking away.

Isaac grabbed her arm. "Why so huffy, Mighty?"

"He just seemed nice, that's all."

"Obviously you thought so."

"Obviously?"

Isaac was really beginning to annoy her.

"I clomped up behind you loud as a herd of mustangs and ya never so much as looked around." He grinned at her. "Did you get his name?"

"Oh, really, Isaac. You're so vexing."

"Well, did you?"

She made a face. "Kane Braxton."

"Kane Braxton?"

"You've heard of him?"

"Heck no. What kind of name is that? Kane Braxton!"

"A very elegant name, if you ask me," Jane said, lifting a belligerent brow.

"Well, it sounds phony to me. Now if it was Joe or Sam, but *Kane*. . .and *Braxton*. I'll bet you a penny for a dime he made it up." Isaac folded his arms and leaned back against the pillar of the overhang, laughing at her.

"Well, if he stays, you can ask him," she said over her shoulder as she turned away in disgust.

"Hey, wait a minute." He grabbed her arm again. "I'm on a mission. Don't get yer dander up; it's not for me. It's for Ma."

Jane turned. "Is everything all right?"

"Never better," he added smugly, "now that she has her baby back."

"Ha, ha!"

"Wish you felt as grateful." He crossed his arms and gave her a beleaguered look.

Jane sighed. "Get on with it, Minstrel Man."

"Ma says she hasn't seen you in a bit. She misses you. Wants you to come up for supper." He grinned at her. "Wear your sidearm. In case anyone's lookin' they'll think you're on official business."

It was true. A decent lady in those parts wasn't seen entering a saloon. Even the sheriff! She usually left that chore to her deputy if she could.

"Everybody knows by now I'm there to see my friend, Jackie Lee, not liquor up." Jane turned and stuck her head back through the office door. "Hey, Spike, I'll be up at the saloon if you need me."

"Official business?"

"No, social."

eight

Jackie Lee let out a squeal of delight when she saw Jane. "I'm so glad you came, dear girl," she cried, her golden pompadour bouncing as she drew Jane into the large, wood-planked saloon.

"Oh, my." Jane stood back and clapped her hands. "Jackie Lee, what a transformation."

By the window, a couple of Ludd Morgan's cowhands, playing poker with Fred Apple and his cousin Herb, glanced up in surprise to see a woman in the saloon. Even the sheriff. At the bar, Otis Dengle slid deeper onto his stool, casting Jane a skittish glance.

"Don't worry, Otis, I'm not here on official business."

It was early yet.

"I thought you'd be impressed." Jackie Lee's proud smile was brighter than any of the hanging lamps lighting the scattered gaming tables.

The rough-hewn pine walls had been painted a warm celadon that neutralized the viridescent green on the pool table in the rear. Plaid tartan chair cushions matched the pleated valance above the front window. Unlike the days when old Jake August was alive, the room was bright and clean. The brass footrail and the mahogany counter were polished to a high sheen, and, most notably, the picture of the naked lady behind the bar had been replaced by a placid pastoral scene.

"I declare," Jane pronounced. "It looks more like a posh gentleman's club than a small-town saloon."

Isaac smirked. "As if you knew what a posh gentleman's club looked like."

"All right, smarty, how a posh gentleman's club should look," Jane said with a toss of her curls.

"I finally convinced Ma to get rid of the lace curtains," Isaac said.

"And the pink spittoons." Jane laughed, noting the handsome polished brass ones at intervals along the bar.

"Why, I never had pink spittoons," Jackie Lee exclaimed.

"No, but Otis claimed they were coming next."

"That Otis!" Jackie Lee cast a weary look over her shoulder.

Jane knew Jackie Lee could have said much more about the man, but she didn't believe in speaking ill of her clients, and he was one of her best.

"Otis had a point, Ma, admit it. If not paintin' 'em pink you were ready to turn 'em into planters."

"Such a nasty habit." Jackie Lee wrinkled her pretty nose.

Not only had the saloon been transformed, but so had Jackie Lee. Jane would hardly have recognized her as the beaten-down woman who had once dragged around town.

"Look what else," Jackie Lee said, drawing Jane across the room. "Ta da!" She threw open the door to an enclosed alcove. Six small square tables had been set with linen tablecloths and napkins, flowers, and fine cutlery.

"I wanted to use some of the nice things I'd inherited from my mama," Jackie Lee confided.

"And why not?" Jane said enthusiastically.

Why not if it made a sweet lady happy? But in a saloon?

"The eatery Ma has always dreamed of. She had me open up that door to the outside." Isaac pointed to a door in the corner. "So folks don't have to come through the saloon."

"And I can close this one," Jackie Lee added as she demonstrated, "for privacy."

If only Jackie Lee had had the faith to turn the whole place into a lovely eatery. For sure, the good Lord would have helped her out, Jane thought.

"Ma happens to be one terrific cook. Why, Cotton Smather has ridden clear out from his farm three times this week to eat Ma's vittles," Isaac said.

"And he doesn't drink," Jackie Lee added.

"This has been going on right under my nose." Jane shook her head. "I can't believe it."

"It's only been a week and a half since we finished." Jackie Lee looked fondly at her son. "Since my boy came home to help me." She smiled at Jane. "You've had other things on your mind, like keeping the peace when old Ludd Morgan's in town and schoolhouses burning down and such."

"Well, that's true enough. It has been a busy week," Jane agreed. "But still, Spike's been up here on his nightly rounds. You'd have thought he'd have told me."

"He can keep his mouth shut when he wants to," Jackie Lee said. "We let him in on the surprise."

Isaac grinned. "Tell her about Ladies' Night, Ma."

Jackie Lee smiled.

"Ma is encouragin' the boys to treat their wives to a night out. First time last night."

"Here?" Jane asked, incredulous.

Isaac nodded. "They came in through the side entrance, of course. She insists the boys act courteous, like gentlemen to their wives."

"I make the ones in the saloon behave, too, while the ladies are dining. Figure it won't hurt 'em for an hour. If they can't, I'll just have Isaac toss 'em out on their ear," Jackie Lee said.

Isaac chuckled. "If you ask me, Ma's well on her way to reformin' Pa's old clients."

Jackie Lee shrugged. "It's good for 'em to have to behave for a change. And those with wives, it helps the marriages. The good Lord knows most of them can use it."

Isaac smiled at his mother. "Ma is a missionary at heart."

"It's the least I can do. These men coming in here, leaving the missus and the little ones alone nights is trial enough for those poor souls. Nobody knows that better than I do." She shook her head sadly. "There's lots about this business that I hate, but I think I hate that the most."

A determined look came into her eye. "Once I pay off Jake August's debts, which will take a spell, I intend to get rid of that old bar and make this a fine eating house."

Jane prayed her friend's ragged faith would be made strong enough not to wait.

"Ya won't make as much money," Isaac pointed out.

Some help you are, Isaac!

"But I'll be a happier woman." Jackie Lee wiped her eyes with the flounced corner of her apron and sniffed.

Isaac put his arm around her. "It'll happen, Ma." He glanced over at the bar. "And with your fine cookin' I reckon you'll keep even your present customers. They'll just have to find another place to do their drinkin'." He grinned down at her. "That is, if you haven't converted them into sobriety by then."

Jackie Lee gave Isaac a tearful smile and looked at Jane. "Do you think the fine folks in town will want to come? I mean, like the Figgs and the Warners and the like. . .seeing this is still a saloon, and all."

"Of course they will. If the vittles are as good as Isaac claims, word'll spread and folks will realize you're serious about turning the saloon into a proper place to dine."

Jane would make it her business they came, if she had to handcuff every one of them and drag them in personally.

Isaac patted Jackie Lee's shoulder. "My belly is howlin', Ma. What's for supper?"

"Well. . ." Jackie Lee slid her hands into the oversized pockets of her ruffled white apron. "The menu this evening is a small bowl of tomato soup for starters, beef stew with carrots and potatoes, snap beans, and biscuits."

"What about dessert?"

"Apple pie."

"À la mode, I hope."

"Really, Isaac," Jane interjected, "you're shameless."

"Not at all." Jackie Lee jumped to her son's defense. "Creek has been turning the ice cream for the last hour."

"Creek's Ma's piano player now."

"Creek Rivers?" Jane asked, astounded.

Jackie Lee nodded. "You probably didn't know Creek was a

classically trained musician, before he turned to drink."

"He's sober now," Isaac said, "thanks to Ma. Once she'd shown him Jesus. One of Ma's miracles."

"I'll say," Jane agreed. "I wondered what happened to him." There was a time when Creek Rivers was practically a permanent resident of Whispering Bluff jail. Not that he did anything very sinful, other than disturbing the peace.

Maybe that was Jackie Lee's purpose for now. Being an instrument of God's love and mercy for folks like Creek.

"He's even taken to writing religious tracts," Isaac said. "Leaves them on top of the piano in case somebody's interested."

"Is anyone ever?" Jane asked. She couldn't imagine.

"They went real fast on Ladies' Night." Jackie Lee smiled.

"Ma's hoping to sober up the whole bunch by the time she makes this into an eatery." Isaac gave his mother an affectionate hug.

"Ladies invading their private domain? That in itself should have a sobering effect." Jane laughed, then turned a solemn gaze on Jackie Lee. "With your mama's faith, Isaac, and her renewed spirit, I wouldn't put anything past her." She looked up at Isaac. "You know what it says in the Bible about moving mountains."

Jackie Lee's face was pensive. " 'If ye have faith as a grain of mustard seed, ye shall say unto this mountain, Remove hence to yonder place; and it shall remove; and nothing shall be impossible unto you.' "

If only Jackie Lee had been able to move that mountain that was her husband.

Only the occasional chink of silver dollars from the poker tables intruded on that quiet, thoughtful moment between the three of them.

"My stomach's still grumblin', Ma," Isaac reminded her.

"I'm sorry. Of course!" Jackie Lee fluttered to a table against the wall, indicating a chair for Jane, which Isaac pulled out for her.

"I'm helping," Jane said, ignoring his gallantry.

"Oh, no you're not, my dear. Everything's done. Just a few last-minute details and that's what I have Maria for."

Jane smiled at the pretty, dark-haired young woman now standing in the doorway, her hands neatly folded over her starched apron, her laced black boots primly together beneath the hem of her ankle-length tartan skirt.

"Very well." With a shrug and a sigh, Jane lowered herself into the chair.

As she waited to be served, Jane surveyed the charming little room. At least here Jackie Lee had her lace curtains. Someday, when her dream was fully realized, this would be a truly special place, with candlelight and soft music, instead of the boisterous conversation of whiskey drinkers. Where ladies could come with fine gentlemen with golden hair and silver eyes, and—

"You're dreamin', Jane. You haven't touched your soup."

"Oh, I'm sorry."

Such a lovely dream.

nine

Walking through the woods the next afternoon on the way to visit her friend Mary Aubrey, Jane reflected on her evening with Isaac and Jackie Lee. She had always known how much Isaac loved his mama, but with that mean old papa of his bent on wrecking every moment of happiness, he had been given scant chance to show her. Now he seemed intent on making up for all those wasted years. Seeing him so tender with his mama, Jane could imagine how sweetly he would someday treat his wife.

She smiled as she ran her fingers lightly along the thicket of pin cherries on the right side of the path.

And then there was that ugly old saloon! What Jackie Lee had done with it was nothing short of a miracle. Even the outside looked spruced up, with the pots of grape holly climbing up the front posts and over the door. And the elegance inside—marred only by the stench of tobacco smoke. And that sweet little eating area. Why, she'd transformed that room into a real showplace with its side entrance, striped awning, and flowers painted around the door so it would bloom even in winter. And her dream of a fine restaurant.

Jane sighed. She wondered, as Jackie Lee had, how many of the good townsfolk would patronize the place. But that's where faith came in.

She plucked a pin cherry along the path and examined it. It was already beginning to turn pink. Wouldn't be long before they'd be ripe for eating.

Big Jim.

She wondered if he had gotten wind of the changes. Him not being a drinker, there'd be no way unless someone told him. And he didn't come into town all that often. One thing for sure, he might not imbibe, but he did have a big appetite. Jane had seen that firsthand at church socials. Now that Jackie Lee had created that lovely new alcove and was featuring food, he should be told.

And I know just the person to tell him, Jane thought, hopping over a branch that had fallen across the path.

Me!

She leaned over to examine an especially fat green worm and straightened.

He'll be real grateful, too, him being a bachelor.

Jane could certainly vouch for the vittles. Of course, as far as Big Jim was concerned, whatever Jackie Lee served would hardly matter. He was a kick-the-sand, callow youth when it came to that woman. She could serve dirt and he'd call it delicious.

Yes, indeed, Big Jim Houston would be right grateful. And not just because of the food!

Jane had no doubt, now that a suitable time had gone by since Jake August had passed, the shy man would be searching for a seemly way to approach his beloved Jackie Lee. And Jane would give him his opportunity.

She pushed aside a cobweb that was hanging from the branch of the gambel oak above her.

Yes, she decided, the first step in helping Jackie Lee's dream come true—and Big Jim's, too—was to tell him about the little eating alcove in Jackie Lee's saloon.

She leaned back against the trunk of a mulberry tree and crossed her arms, allowing her mind to drift.

Oh, how she wished she had her own Big Jim.

Ever since she'd lost Peter Chaloupek to Becca, and then John Aubrey to dear Mary—a much better match she had to admit—she'd wondered if she ever would find her own true love. She'd always been so sure God had someone special waiting to capture her heart and cherish and love her, as she knew her friends were cherished and loved. But as time had gone by and no prince had reared his handsome head, she'd gotten more and more discouraged.

Would she end up a bitter spinster, like the Pryce sisters? Or even worse, like the mayor's secretary, Lilly Johnson, who imagined every man was after her in an unseemly way when he innocently tipped his hat.

She didn't want to be so hungry for love that even a mysterious stranger could set her heart pounding and make her palms grow moist. Which, to her chagrin, was exactly what had happened the evening before.

She lifted her denim skirt as she took the path's right fork, veering toward the creek, her shortcut to Mary's house.

The stranger, Kane Braxton, had been intruding on her thoughts continually since he'd left her behind at the corner of Main and First and disappeared behind Norwood's bank. More than once she'd replayed the moment when he'd accosted her in the twilight, right there in front of the sheriff's office.

Perhaps "accost" was too extreme. . .and "twilight" a bit too romantic.

But in remembering, that's how it seemed—or how she wanted it to seem.

And now, as she made her way through the strip of woods that backed up on the little town, stepping over the mossy rocks, crossing the chuckling creek, she even imagined she heard his rich Southern drawl.

"Good afternoon, Miss Sheriff."

She even imagined him on the other side of the creek, lounging languidly against the trunk of a lanceleaf cottonwood in his dove-gray cutaway and pinstriped trousers, looking very much the city gentleman, his gray eyes casting their gaze across at her like two silver bullets, straight at her heart.

"Are you checkin' on me, Miss Sheriff? I don't see your gun."

She would have slipped into the creek had he not leaped up and caught her.

"What are you doing here?" she sputtered, melting in his grasp.

"Should I not be? I was under the impression that this was public land."

"It is, but. . ."

She felt the burn of his hands even through the sturdy denim of her blouse.

"But?" He tilted his head, his smile expectant, amused.

"But you surprised me."

He was even taller than she'd imagined, and his shoulders broader. She glanced down at his hands, still circling her wrists. His hands, strong but gentler than she might have expected, with long, tapering fingers and neatly trimmed nails. A gentleman's hands!

Catching her breath, she pulled away, peeking up beneath her lashes.

"I'm stayin' at Miss Trudy's boardinghouse, like you so kindly recommended last night," he said.

It took her a moment before she could gather her wits to reply. "I—I hope it's satisfactory," she murmured, stepping back on an unsteady foot and clasping her trembling hands behind her.

She warmed in his appreciative regard as his eyes roamed from the top of her curls, over her modest cape, to the tip of her tooled boots.

His voice was husky when he spoke, thick and honeyed. "I apologize, dear lady, if I've made you uncomfortable. But, without a doubt, you are the prettiest little thing I've seen since Christmas, and I am quite at a loss for words."

"On the contrary, sir," she replied softly, her poise slowly returning. "I'd say you were quite eloquent." His candor was disconcerting, but the earnestness in his tone had given her a heady surge of courage.

His Stetson lay on the grass beside the tree where he had lingered, and in this dappled shade, his hair glowed shiny as a gold coin, his sculpted features burnished by the sunlight.

She saw fine lines around his mouth and creases of laughter edging his eyes. His silver eyes, not bold, but wise and knowing, confirmed what she had first suspected. He was a man of worldly experience.

He cleared his throat. "I can see I'm keeping you."

"Well, no. . .but, yes. I must be on my way. My friend is expecting me. She lives in the cottage over there." Jane inclined her head.

"With the arbor of roses."

"Wait until you see them in bloom."

"If I stay so long." He smiled. "I noticed the house on my morning walk. Charming."

"Mary will be happy to hear you think so. Her garden is her pride and joy. Her husband John is the schoolmaster, you know. Though why would you? You having just arrived." His fixed attention had made her giddy.

"I can see you are a font of information, Miss Sheriff. Do you suppose, one day you could do me the honor of a tour?"

"I'm sure, sir." Jane gave him a coy smile. "Perhaps, as a newcomer, you might enjoy the church potluck supper Wednesday evening."

"Potluck?"

She laughed. "Don't worry, all you need bring is your appetite. The ladies cook, the men eat."

"That sounds like an irresistible offer."

"Good Shepherd Community Church. Five o'clock. And now I must be off."

He took Jane's hand and lowered his golden head. She felt the gentle brush of his mustache and the soft touch of his lips. . . and his warm breath caress her wrist.

He straightened, half-smiling, an invitation in his eyes.

Prodded by her conscience to flee such temptation, Jane tossed her curls and whirled around, feeling the heat of his gaze as she hurried down the path. Only when she knew she was beyond his sight did she slow.

Kane Braxton was obviously a man of culture and refinement, from his well-spoken accent to the fine cut of his clothes. Despite his expressed intentions, she doubted he'd be long in this little town.

Clearly he was a man of passionate inclinations. If she had a lick of sense, or one speck of backbone, she would stay clear of him. But if not, while he was here she must be on her guard at all times. She must not allow herself, for even a single second, to be unduly seduced by his charming ways.

Such a man could only break a girl's heart. And her poor ragged heart had no more room for patches.

≈

Kane Braxton watched the little sheriff trip down the path like some woodland nymph, dancing among the rays of sunlight filtering through the overhanging branches, her bright curls bobbing, her tiny boots barely touching the ground.

He watched until her blue cape disappeared behind a mountain lilac.

She had a beguiling innocence and a sweetness that left his jaded heart quite spinning.

The tenure of his stay in Whispering Bluff might very well depend on that adorable little person.

Yes, indeed!

ten

It was Wednesday afternoon. Jane slipped into the dress she was wearing to the potluck supper that night and assessed her reflection in the freestanding mirror in her bedroom.

Although she certainly had been told she was pretty—most recently by the handsome stranger—she did not see herself as remarkable. Her short blond curls were decidedly unruly, and she wouldn't have minded at all being a few inches taller.

Her eyes were her most unusual feature, large and slightly lifted at the corners, with long sweeping lashes—her mama's eyes, Papa said. She had been forced to lower them modestly more than once when a newly smitten swain had exclaimed, "Your eyes are *really blue!*"

Their blueness was the reason she had selected this particular dress, a sapphire linen she'd created herself, with a softly pleated bodice and fashionable leg-o'-mutton sleeves.

She cinched the wide belt until her waist was small enough for a man's hands to circle, and thought of Kane Braxton's hands, long-fingered and strong, grasping her wrists when she had almost slipped into the creek.

Was that just yesterday?

Speaking of Kane Braxton!

Humming absently, she twirled about the room, the hem of her gored skirt swinging above her patent leather lace-up shoes. Closing her eyes, she imagined a golden head bending toward her, strong arms holding her close, dancing step to step in perfect harmony.

She sighed.

Suddenly, she stopped and her eyes flew open.

Good heavens! What was wrong with her? She'd spoken to the man twice. Briefly. And here she was, acting like some dotty adolescent instead of a twenty-four-year-old sheriff.

"Get hold of yourself, girl!" she admonished her image in the mirror. "You know nothing about this Kane Braxton. He could very well be—most probably is—a man of more experience than virtue." She shook her head regretfully. "Which is likely what makes him so attractive."

But at church that afternoon, as she went about her committee chores in preparation for the potluck supper, the man, himself, kept intruding into her thoughts.

Would Kane Braxton come to the potluck supper? Certainly, his expression seemed to hold such a promise when he'd kissed her hand and gazed into her eyes.

Well, she supposed she'd learn soon enough.

The fellowship hall was a large, rectangular room in the church basement with soft blue painted walls brightened by numerous hanging kerosene lamps. Kitty-corner from the kitchen was a small stage, and on the wall opposite, years ago Becca's mama had painted a mural of Jesus, suffering the little children to come unto Him.

Isaac and John Aubrey had volunteered to help Pastor Pike set out the sawhorses and planks for the tables. As they lined up the benches on either side for seating, Jane and the potluck committee, consisting of the minister's wife, Pru Pike, Mavis Dodd, and Eunice Figg, followed along behind spreading checkered tablecloths. Behind them a very self-important eight-year-old, Suzie Pike, and other members of the Sunday school, set pots of paper flower centerpieces they'd made, in the middle of each table.

Eunice Figg, wearing one of her remarkable hats—a taxidermied white dove with its feathers spreading over the brim and a silk daisy in its beak—directed the entire operation with her usual dictatorial efficiency. Despite her uppity ways the mayor's rawboned wife could always be counted on to do her share.

If not always to be charitable, Jane thought, noting the woman's expression when Jackie Lee hurried in and handed

Pru her contribution to the potluck supper.

"Oh, Jackie Lee, it's so beautiful, we'll make it the center-piece of the buffet table," Pru insisted as the three committee members gathered around to admire the impressive platter of tomatoes layered in aspic, topped with mayonnaise and garnished with capers and sliced pickles, in a bed of ruffled lettuce.

"It looks too good to eat," Mavis said.

"My goodness, Jackie Lee," Jane said, "you brought enough to feed an army."

"Very nice." Eunice sniffed.

Before she could turn away Jane added, "A taste of what folks can expect in your little alcove eatery, I reckon."

"Alcove eatery?" Mavis asked.

"In a saloon?" Eunice's expression shriveled like a prune, appalled.

Even Pru, the pastor's wife, showed restrained surprise.

When Jackie Lee looked as if she was about to bolt, Jane grabbed her arm. "It's in the same building as the saloon, but entirely separate. It even has its own lovely entry on the side."

"It's still in a saloon," Eunice muttered and then did turn away.

So much for Christian charity!

Jane's gaze followed the woman as she crossed the room. Well, the seed was planted. That's all Jane could do for now. Eunice would come around eventually. She had before.

"I must go now." Jackie Lee disengaged her arm from Jane's grasp.

"Can't you stay?" Pru asked. "Just a little while?"

Sweet Mavis took her hand. "We really wish you would, Jackie Lee. We really mean it."

"That's kind," Jackie Lee said but gently withdrew. "Not tonight." She glanced nervously in Eunice Figg's direction. "Maybe next time."

"We'll hold you to it," Pru said warmly, giving the woman a hug.

Just as Jackie Lee was hurrying out the door, Peter Chaloupek strode in with Big Jim Houston.

"We're here to work," Peter called out.

Jane held her breath, watching as Jackie Lee paused for an instant beside Big Jim then hurried on without meeting his gaze, her head lowered, her hands clasped tightly in front of her ruffled apron.

Big Jim, whose broad, friendly face had creased into a tentative smile at the sight of her, looked like somebody had stuck a pin in him. All the joy escaped as his gaze followed his beloved with such a sorrowful expression it just tore at Jane's heart.

She hurried up as if she hadn't noticed. "Welcome, Big Jim."

"Thank you, Miss Sheriff. Happy to be here." Though at the moment he didn't look it.

"And, Peter," Jane said, turning her attention to his companion. "Where's your papa-in-law?"

The sturdy, black-haired young man set his hat on a nearby table. "Jacob's low with a bout of arthritis. He was real disappointed he couldn't come."

"I'm sorry to hear that."

Isaac came up behind Jane, clamping his big paw on her shoulder as he reached for Peter's hand. "Howdy, partner."

Peter pumped his hand, returning his grin.

Big Jim had begun to circulate as more folks arrived: families with children; widows; the town spinsters, Henrietta and Hazel Pryce with Miss Lilly; and a smattering of single cowboys and farmers like Big Jim and Cotton Smather.

"Doc Warner's wife just arrived," Peter observed. "No doubt with her standby carrot and raisin salad."

Isaac rolled his eyes.

"Don't complain unless you cook," Jane said, turning toward the kitchen.

Over the din Pastor Pike called, "Isaac, come on over with your guitar and entertain the young ones."

Isaac obliged, drawing a stool up onto the little stage where the children scrambled up to gather around him.

Jane smiled, glancing from her friend to the mural of Jesus with the children on the opposite wall. What better example of the Holy Spirit at work in their little church.

Folks were laughing and calling greetings; toddlers were running underfoot chased by anxious mothers; and the youngsters, with Isaac's encouragement, were singing a spirited version of "She'll Be Comin' 'Round the Mountain." The tumult was at its zenith when, in a ringing voice, Pastor Pike called those gathered to a moment of quiet reflection and prayer.

Lowering her eyes, Jane, once again—as she'd done numerous times throughout the last half hour—glanced toward the door, now with a final sense of disappointment.

Just as she'd feared, Kane Braxton wasn't coming after all.

Gradually the room quieted, save for the soft fluttering rustle of the children and the whispered admonitions of their parents.

Pastor Pike began. "Shall we bow our heads. . . ? Dear Lord, we gather this evening to share the bounty of Your blessings. Not only the food on our table but the spiritual food that gives shape and meaning and purpose to our lives. We are grateful, Lord, to be together and for the opportunity to reach out with love and kindness and appreciation for each other. We thank You for the talents You have given to each of us, Lord, and may we put them to good use in spreading Your word and furthering Your work. We ask all this in Jesus' precious name, amen."

As Jane lifted her head, a strange warmth suffused her, and an uncanny premonition. Slowly she turned.

There he stood in the shadows of the threshold, tall, imposing, and handsome as ever she could remember—as ever she could hope for. His mane of gilded hair brushed back behind ears that lay flat and perfect against his sculpted head.

Kane Braxton.

He had come after all.

His gaze scanned the room with increasing concern, a slight frown furrowing his brow.

And then he saw what he had sought, and his face broke into a gleaming smile that split her heart wide open in welcome.

His silver eyes focused only on her as he strode forward, his body loose, languid in its elegance and manly grace. The embroidered waistcoat, the dove-gray cutaway, his legs, long and lean in pale pinstriped trousers...

Was it only *her* breath that caught?

She sensed the room grow quiet as if those who beheld him were also held in sway, as if they, too, understood that they were seeing one who possessed the highest attributes of maleness and manhood.

And he was striding toward her.

Her!

Jane McKee!

eleven

Kane Braxton's gaze was fixed on Jane, insistent in its regard, pulling her toward him, if not physically, with the mesmerizing pull of personality.

"You came after all," she said softly when he reached her.

"I said I would." His eyes smiled down into hers. "I'm a man of my word."

Drowning in quicksilver, that's how it seemed as Jane drew a lingering breath, her brain scrambling for a response.

Pastor Pike came to her rescue. "Welcome, sir," he said, extending his hand. "I don't believe we've met."

"Pastor, this is Kane Braxton," Jane managed to murmur.

The pastor's handshake was hearty. "So, what brings you to these parts, Mr. Braxton?"

"Please call me Kane." He smiled at Jane. "As I explained to your charming sheriff, I thought I'd just stop a spell and see how your town fits."

"Can't do better than Whispering Bluff," Pastor Pike extolled. "There's not a nicer bunch of folks anywhere."

"I'm already beginning to see that," Kane said, his gaze lingering on Jane.

"Let me introduce you around," Pastor Pike offered, taking hold of the man's arm.

Kane cast Jane a rueful smile as he allowed himself to be drawn away.

She smiled back, then with a toss of her curls, turned her attention to passing out biscuits and pleasantries. At the same time, following Kane Braxton's every gesture, straining to hear his honeyed Southern baritone and deep engaging laughter as he progressed from group to group along the rows of tables.

Occasionally he would glance up, and if he caught her watching would wink or send an amused grin—to which she demurely lowered her eyes.

Thrown into such a mix of strangers, most of the young farm boys Jane knew would have been at a loss for words. But Kane Braxton was no simple farm boy; that was obvious from the cut of his clothes to his fine manners. If anything he seemed stimulated, and even more expansive and charming as he tendered small talk with the men and flirted with the ladies—to Jane's vexation.

She felt a poke in her ribs and looked up to discover that Isaac had sidled up beside her. "I'd hate to think your knight might have armor of tin," he whispered.

She almost hit him with the spoon. "What's that supposed to mean?"

He shrugged. "I'm just suggestin' that he might not be all that he appears."

"Is that so?" Jane tilted her head and gave him a decidedly disgusted look. "What you're saying is, instead of a charming, sophisticated gentleman he's really a rough, rude cowboy in disguise." She assessed her friend from the top of his brick-colored hair to the worn toes of his scuffed leather boots. "I don't think so. I'd recognize that type right off. . .and I'm looking at one now."

"Oh, is that so?" Isaac's good-natured grin had turned skeptical. "I'm not blind, Mighty Mite; I saw the way he looked at you. Believe me, there's a predator inside that polished package." He frowned. "But what worries me more is, I saw the way you looked at him."

"Oh, and how was that, Mr. Man-of-Experience?"

"Make light of it if you will." Isaac was quite serious now. "But four years of ridin' the rails and battin' around big cities gave me some insight into character. I just don't cotton to seein' my naive little friend swept off her feet and fallin' into a puddle, heart first."

"Well, thank you very much for your concern," Jane sniffed,

"and your brilliant assessment, seeing as you don't even know him."

"Neither do you."

"Better than you do. You haven't even been introduced."

"Aha," Isaac said, his exuberance returning. "The gauntlet has been thrown. You are absolutely right." He grinned. "Ya see, I am not too stubborn to admit it. Tonight I will make it my business to get acquainted. Startin' now! Here he comes."

Kane was returning with the pastor and as they approached the buffet table, Isaac leaned forward and thrust out his hand. "I don't believe we've met. I'm Isaac August." There was an edge to his voice and his smile. "Janie's protector and childhood friend."

Jane rolled her eyes, sagging with embarrassment. "My *audacious* childhood friend," she said, stomping on Isaac's instep behind the table.

Isaac let out a yelp. "What'd you do that for? Are you tryin' to break my foot?"

"I'd prefer your neck," she muttered.

Kane laughed. "I don't doubt for a minute your winsome friend needs protection," he murmured, "in matters of the heart." He smiled at Jane as he grasped Isaac's hand.

Pastor Pike interrupted. "I think our guest has earned his supper," he said, handing Kane a plate from the end of the buffet table.

Kane scanned the room. "It looks as if just about everyone has been served. Can you join me, Jane?"

"By all means, Janie girl." Isaac circled the table, grabbing a plate for himself and handing one to her. He turned to Kane. "May I suggest the carrot and raisin salad?"

What a hypocrite! Isaac can't stand carrot and raisin salad.

Isaac continued his blithe suggestions, some sincere, as he followed Kane down the line of food, loading his own plate in the process. "Mavis' macaroni and cheese is outstandin'." He also helped himself to a generous portion of the Pryce sisters' fried chicken, which everyone agreed was surprisingly good considering who made it.

"Help yourself to my ma's tomatoes in aspic." He pointed to the gelatinous remains of the once beautiful platter and waited patiently until Kane had no choice but to politely comply. "Ma owns the saloon here in town. One of the showplaces of Whisperin' Bluff." He winked at Jane. "At the end of Main on the lefthand side going out of town." He reached for a piece of lemon meringue pie. "In case you need to wet your whistle."

"Thanks, but I don't drink," Kane said, helping himself to a wedge of chocolate cream pie.

Jane threw Isaac a triumphant smile. "The chocolate cookies are mine," she murmured. "Were mine. There's just one left."

"They must be very popular."

"You bet," Isaac said, his hand shooting out as Kane reached for the cookie.

"That was so rude," Jane muttered to Isaac, throwing him a disgusted look.

"Gee, I thought I was payin' you a compliment, Janie; you know how much I love those cookies." He turned to the newcomer. "Sorry, Kane. Looks like I can never please this girl. She just chastised me again for my bad manners. Here, be my guest." He dropped the rich, chewy disk onto the man's plate.

Kane lifted a sardonic brow. "I wouldn't want to deprive you."

"No, no. I want you to have it," Isaac said with profuse generosity.

"Thank you so much," Kane said, with exaggerated sincerity, putting an end to Isaac's antics.

It was about time!

Betty Jean Gordon was waving from a table in the corner. "Yoo-hoo, Isaac. There's room over here."

At last! Now she would be rid of the boor.

"There are three of us," Isaac called back.

But no such luck.

"We can make room," Betty Jean eagerly assured him,

although Jane couldn't see possibly how. From where she stood the bench already looked crowded.

She should have known better. When it came to Isaac, Betty Jean could always make room.

"Great!" Isaac called, grabbing Jane's plate from her and leaving her and Kane no alternative but to follow him as he wove through the tangle of tables in the crowded hall.

Betty Jean wiggled over, fluttering her long lashes coyly as Isaac plopped Jane's plate down next to his on the checkered tablecloth and squeezed in beside Betty Jean, leaving Kane to gallantly assist Jane over the wooden bench.

What a contrast in manners!

Well, at least Isaac would be occupied with Betty Jean, and Jane would finally be able to talk to Kane without him interrupting and hogging the whole conversation.

But it was not to be.

Isaac had vowed to get acquainted with Kane and nothing, it seemed, not even Betty Jean Gordon's big brown eyes or rosebud pink lips, was going to deter him.

Still, it was not all bad. Squeezed on the bench between Kane and Isaac, tight as tomatoes in a lug, Jane was deliciously aware of the man beside her, the touch of his shoulder, the press of his thigh against hers. . .furtive glances rewarded with a smile.

Even before Isaac had tackled Mavis' macaroni and cheese he leaned forward and began his interrogation.

"So, Kane, where did you come from?"

"Originally?" Kane, who had thoughtfully poured each of the three of them a glass of lemonade, returned the pitcher to the center of the table.

"That's a good place to start." Isaac popped a bite of casserole into his mouth.

"Well, I grew up in North Carolina," Kane began, his soft Southern drawl attesting to his heritage. "Went to the North Carolina College of Agriculture and Mechanic Arts."

"You're a college man."

Kane nodded.

"What did you study?"

"Back then I was considering becoming a teacher. Then my grandpa passed and left me a small inheritance. I was still wet behind the ears, as I look back. A young fella. . .about your age—"

Young fella! I love it! That should put Isaac in his place.

Kane continued, "Thought I'd do a bit of travelin' before I settled down."

"By boat I reckon, not boxcar," Isaac muttered.

"I beg your pardon?"

"Nothin'. Go on."

"I traveled around Europe a couple of years. Got homesick for America. On the ship, returnin', I met an older chap—we really hit it off. He was into buying and selling commodities. When we got back, he took me under his wing, taught me the ropes. Turned out I was pretty good at it, if I do say so myself. And lucky!" He scooped his first forkful of carrot and raisin salad. "That's about it."

But before the fork could reach his mouth, Isaac had another question.

"That doesn't explain what you're doin' here in Whisperin' Bluff."

"Oh, Isaac." Jane frowned. "Will you let the man eat? Besides, he's already explained that."

"Not to me."

Kane gave Jane an indulgent smile. "I think your protector wants to be sure I'm legitimate." He put down his fork and addressed Isaac. "A couple of years ago I realized I wasn't getting any younger. I'd made a lot of money, but what did I have to show for it? I started travelin', searchin' for a place to settle down, buy some land. . . . Maybe start a family." He was silent for a moment, as if turning things over in his mind. "I've been looking over towns along the way. This one just seemed to draw me in." Then he smiled at Jane, as if to say it was she as much as the town that had attracted him.

Or was that just her wishful imagination?

She lowered her gaze then glanced over at Isaac. The frown on his face told her he had read Kane's smile the same.

"So here I am," Kane said. "Can't say what will happen next. I expect the Lord will let me know." He shrugged, shoved the forkful of carrot and raisin salad into his mouth, chewed, and swallowed. "That's my story." He gave Isaac a level look. "Does that satisfy you?"

Isaac didn't reply, returning Kane's steady regard.

"I figure I've gotten past needing to prove anything," Kane added quietly.

Unlike some people I know, Jane thought with an irritated glance toward Isaac.

Isaac was spared a response when Pastor Pike stepped up onto the small stage and clapped for attention. When the room quieted, he said, "What do you say we have Isaac come up here with his guitar and lead us in some singing?"

There was a round of encouraging applause as Isaac rose, but none more encouraging than Jane's. At last she would be free of her friend's intrusive presence. Free to bask in the singular admiration of the handsome man beside her.

As Kane's smile enveloped her, she shivered with the thrill of awareness.

Isaac touched her shoulder as he rose and waved good-naturedly to the crowd. "Only if the kids'll help me out," he called, making his way through the labyrinth of tables.

Jane smiled and shook her head, watching the children cluster around him, the young ones leaning up against him, the older ones gathering at his feet.

Isaac showed off his skill with a few intricate arpeggios, then strummed a couple of simple chords and began to sing a rousing "Stand Up, Stand Up for Jesus." Soon everyone joined in.

Timmy Aubrey sidled up and pulled on his sleeve. Isaac leaned down and the child whispered in his ear. Nodding, he straightened then raised his hand for attention. "Timmy and I have a duet. You tell them, Timmy."

Timmy had lifted his shy, uncertain gaze. " 'All Things

Bright and Beautiful,'" came the small, wavering voice.

The notes throbbed from Isaac's scarred guitar, mellow and pure, as together, he and Timmy began.

When they had finished, a prolonged silence fell over the room.

Then Eunice Figg sniffed.

Big Jim pulled a large red handkerchief out of his vest pocket and unashamedly wiped his eyes.

Suddenly, the Widow Mott's grandbaby let out a great wail in her mother's arms, and pandemonium broke loose. Joyous applause enveloped the room as very solemnly Isaac rose and, side-by-side, he and Timmy took a deep and formal bow.

When he straightened, a smile wreathed Isaac's face. One hand held his guitar; the other rested on Timmy's slender shoulder. "I wish the fellowship hall had a piano. If you think this boy can sing, you should hear him play the piano." He laughed. "Anybody want to donate one?"

There was a smattering of laughter and then surprised silence when next to Jane, a mellow, masculine voice, with a soft, Southern cadence called out, "I'd consider it an honor to present a piano to this fine little church."

twelve

Kane had insisted on staying to help clean up after the potluck. But despite his intentions, he was constantly sidetracked by the cluster of congregants thanking him for his generous promise of a piano for the fellowship hall.

It was obvious to Jane that what they really wanted to do was to get better acquainted with the handsome newcomer. Especially since most of them were single girls—and their assertive mamas.

While Isaac and Peter swept the floor and lined up the tables and benches for classes the next day, and Jane, along with the other committee members, removed the soiled tablecloths and washed and stacked the dishes, she watched with a sinking heart as the gaggle of pretty young girls giggled and flirted with Kane. And he, ever the gentleman, did not disappoint them but responded with the same charm that had won her.

They knew a good man when they saw one. And one as handsome and suave, as charming—and obviously affluent—as Kane Braxton did not ride into Whispering Bluff every day. If ever!

Isaac's playful pokes and teasing, the veiled *I warned you* expression in his eyes, only made matters worse, and by the time Pastor Pike turned down the kerosene lamps she was feeling about as low as she could remember.

She was sure that now that Kane had been exposed to Whispering Bluff's society, he would be swept up into a round of picnics and dinners and invitations, and it was doubtful he'd ever take a second look at a woman law officer.

Loves longed for and lost seemed to be her luck.

She sighed as she lifted her cape from a hook on the cloakroom wall.

Suddenly, a hand reached from behind her and took it. Kane's strong, slim fingers grasped the collar of her cloak, and when she turned he placed it ever so gently over her shoulders. Her breath caught as he bent toward her, his honeyed voice soft and intimate. "I've been waiting to walk you home, Miss Sheriff."

Going suddenly shy, she glanced up and met his warm gaze. . .and shivered. The delicious thought of a moonlight walk in the whispering breeze, rich with the scent of spring blossoms, sent tingles skittering up her spine.

But before she could respond, a voice boomed in her ear, "Time to head home, Mighty Mite. They're closin' down the place." Isaac grabbed hold of her arm as if he owned her.

For a moment she was struck dumb, then furious. Didn't he see Kane standing beside her, leaning toward her, whispering in her ear?

Of course he did! That was the point.

"This is a church, Isaac. It doesn't close down like your mama's old saloon." She yanked her arm from his grasp.

Isaac drew back in surprise. A hurt expression passed across his face, and then embarrassment.

Immediately she was bathed in guilt for her insulting words—and angry with Isaac for pushing her to the point of saying them.

She had not asked him to be her protector. All night he had deliberately interfered, monopolized the conversation, been brash, and downright rude to Kane. And now, it was almost as if he had been lying in wait, to pounce and ruin the rest of the evening.

Still, the words that had flown from her lips had been personal and demeaning, and she was sorry.

Sighing, she murmured, "I didn't mean it, Isaac."

"Mean what, sweetie pie?"

Pretending he didn't notice. That was Isaac. Which made her even more ashamed.

Kane took her arm as they climbed the basement steps

behind Isaac and the rest of the committee and gathered outside, exchanging good-byes as they dispersed into the starlit night.

Which was wasted now, as Isaac fell into step on the other side of Jane.

What could she do? It was his route home, too.

"Beautiful night," Isaac observed. "Full moon." He turned to Jane. "Do you realize it's been almost a month since the fire? It was over there," he said to Kane, pointing toward the northeast. "Big ball a orange shot above the trees. It was beautiful and horrifyin' all at once. Schoolhouse burned to the ground by the time we got there. Children are usin' the fellowship hall till the town can afford to build another one."

"Jane told me," Kane murmured.

"Lucky we had a place big enough to accommodate 'em all. Course, they're havin' to make do, but kids are resilient."

Isaac was droning on in a soliloquy of his own, hardly pausing to breathe, not waiting for a response. Apparently not noticing that Kane had quietly taken Jane's arm and was gently helping her over the ruts and potholes in the rough street, and casting her warm glances that held admiration and promise.

Not noticing or choosing to ignore.

Jane marched silently between them, feeling the pressure of Kane's arm, the rhythm of his step, and wishing with every stride that dear Isaac would be sucked up into the stratosphere.

Would he never be quiet?

Would he never be gone?

Couldn't he tell by her silence that she wanted it so? Why was he being so obtuse?

As they approached her cottage they slowed, and she thought for sure he would move on.

But no! As Kane assisted her up the steps of her little rose-covered veranda, Isaac, too, bounded up. He leaned back against the balustrade, crossing his ankles, his arms akimbo, fixed to stay as long as it took. "You never said the towns you've been to, Kane. I'm curious." Beginning his interrogation again, as if hours hadn't passed in between. . .as if Jane weren't even there.

She could feel her ire rising again, and for the first time, she sensed Kane's disquiet.

"I think you two gentlemen should have supper together," she said abruptly. "Maybe you could invite Kane for one of your mama's fine meals, Isaac. Just the two of you! Then you could ask him all the questions you want."

She took a deep breath. "In the meantime, I will say good night!"

Suddenly Isaac was all apologies, though she didn't believe it for a second. "Oh, I'm so sorry, Janie. Of course, we should have been more sensitive."

We?

"You must be mighty tired, sheriffin' all day and headin' up the potluck committee that way. And I'll bet you have a big day tomorrow, too. You're right! Kane and I should be on our way."

But Kane didn't let go of her arm. "You go on," he said, moving aside to make it easy for Isaac to get past.

"I want to talk to Miss Janie about taking me on the tour she promised."

"Tour?" Isaac asked jovially. "That sounds like a good idea. I wouldn't mind joinin' in on that. See what the area looks like since I left."

"No need, Isaac," Jane snapped. "The prairie is still there, the mountains are still there. Rikum's Pond is still there."

"Speakin' of Rikum's Pond—and promises. . ." Ignoring her tone, Isaac had settled back again. "When are we goin' fishin', like you promised *me*? How about tomorrow mornin'? Early! Say five thirty?" He turned to the other man. "Maybe you'd like to join us, Kane."

What is Isaac up to?

"I don't think so," Kane said evenly. Releasing her arm, he looked down at Jane. "I guess you and I can talk about our tour some other time."

"No! Now is as good a time as any." Boldly Jane grabbed Kane's sleeve. "We can go tomorrow. If you like. I'll show you the Craig farm. It's a real fine piece of land in the high plains at the foot of the hills. Old Man Craig's been muttering about him and the missus being too old to keep it up. Could be he'd sell it if the price was right. That is, if someone was interested."

She turned to Isaac. "As for our fishing expedition, Rikum's Pond will still be there next week. We can discuss it then. Good night, Isaac. Be sure to tell your mama what a hit her tomatoes in aspic were." Jane pursed her lips and glared at him, even though she knew he couldn't see her clearly in the dark of the covered porch.

Isaac cleared his throat. "Well, ah. . .all right then." He pushed himself upright. "Guess I'll be off." Instead of going down the steps he swung over the balustrade onto the grass.

"G'night all," he called with a brief salute, then shoved his hands into his pockets and with a jaunty swagger, strode up the street.

Jane and Kane stood on the veranda listening to his whistle fade into the darkness.

She was the first to break their silence. "Perhaps I'll make a picnic. Would you like that?"

"Very much," Kane said, squeezing her hand. He held it long enough. . .longer than necessary, until he reluctantly released it. "Well then, I'll say good night." At the bottom of the steps he paused. "What time shall I pick you up?"

Jane stood in the quiet darkness, gazing down at the figure in front of her, bathed in the pale glow of the moon. He was so tall, so very tall, if she reached out she could touch his silvery hair, run her fingers through the soft waves brushing from his brow.

Oh, she prayed the sound of her thudding heart did not reach his ears as it so clearly resounded in hers.

She stood for a moment, considering the things she would prepare to tempt his appetite.

"Eleven o'clock," she said. "That will give me time."

Isaac's whistling sounded as hollow to himself as he was sure it did to Jane and Kane, a blustering bravado to hide his embarrassment.

He kicked up a clod of dirt.

Danged if he hadn't made a fool of himself, yammering away as if a steam engine was attached to his mouth. And now he had Janie mad at him, real mad. Even though he couldn't see her expression in the dark, he'd felt the heat, all right.

But doggone it, he couldn't help it. He had a feelin' about that Kane Braxton fella, like an itch that he couldn't reach to scratch. A real strong feelin', and it wasn't a good one. It was the kind one man gets about another. Call it instinct.

It wasn't that the man had done anything bad. On the contrary, he'd been the perfect gentleman—too perfect. That was the problem. Isaac had seen the type before, slick, suave—obsequious. And Jane was drinkin' it up like she'd just found an oasis in the desert.

He dreaded the moment she discovered it was all a mirage. And she would. He was convinced.

He clomped up the stairs to the apartment above the saloon. Instead of going inside he leaned over and crossed his arms on the porch rail, facing out over the creek. Moonlight dripped over the trees like molten silver, the shrubbery dark below. He could smell the woods, and if he listened real careful, above the din of the saloon, he could hear the soft chuckle of the creek.

His ma had told him about Janie's unfortunate romance with Peter when Becca was first away at medical school and havin' a romance of her own. Isaac could have predicted the outcome of that one. Peter and Becca had always been a pair, soul mates. Kinda like him and Jane, but of a more serious nature. And then that John Aubrey came along. Nice fellow, but Ma said it was more on Janie's part than his.

Sweet Janie—she was so trusting, so hopeful. She'd always been that way. Maybe that's why he felt this fierce need to protect her. And now that he was here, if he didn't and she got her heart broken again, he'd feel responsible.

Him responsible?

He frowned, paused for a moment, then shook his head.

Now wasn't that stupid!

It wasn't like Janie was totally wet behind the ears. She was a grown woman, after all. And a sheriff, at that! Where did he think he came off protecting her? She was the one with the gun.

Besides, it wasn't like he was some expert in the love department—despite his past experiences. Instead of looking out after Mighty Mite, who didn't want him to in the first place, maybe he oughta start lookin' out fer himself. Start payin' attention to some of those pretty town girls who were payin' attention to him. Like Betty Jean Gordon, for instance. Maybe he oughta start doin' that, instead of botherin' after somebody who didn't want to be bothered.

He straightened and shoved his hands down into his pockets.

When he'd first come home things just seemed to fall back into their rightful order, like he remembered. He and Janie had understood each other then, the same way as always. Now this Kane fellow had entered the picture and everything seemed to be changing.

It didn't seem right.

thirteen

Jane sprang out of bed as the first fingers of dawn crept across the sill. Her heart was singing even as her feet hit the braided rug. This day was going to be special. She felt it in her bones.

Today she would discover Kane Braxton's dreams and hopes, what he valued and held dear. Today she would plumb the depths of his soul!

She threw open the curtains, lifted the sash, and leaned out the window, checking the cloudless cerulean sky as she breathed in the crisp, morning air, redolent with the scent of roses.

Would he live up to her expectations? Would he have as much substance as charm?

Oh, she truly hoped so.

She cocked her elbow on the sill and rested her chin in her palm, gazing out across Main Street and past the meadow on the south side of the church. Poplar leaves danced and glistened in the early morning breeze, and the faces of wild daises popped up through the spring grasses, tufts of white amid the swaying green blades.

If Kane did decide to stay in Whispering Bluff, what sort of employment would he seek?

Would he buy land and be a *gentleman* farmer? Or would he, as he had intimated, have enough money to settle into a life of more artistic pursuits? Or perhaps philanthropy.

He was very well spoken. Perhaps he would prove to be a man of letters.

Now didn't that sound urbane and sophisticated?

Whatever choice it was would certainly be in keeping with his elegant and gracious manner.

Imagine, being married to a country gentleman who had literary leanings.

Married?

She blushed at the thought of her audacity. She didn't even really know the man.

Still, she thought dreamily, it didn't hurt to imagine.

Across the meadow, just before the rise, she saw a man and a child walking.

She leaned forward, squinting against the light. It was hard to tell. . . . Oh, yes. John Aubrey and Timmy, out for a morning stroll, as they often did.

Children!

What about children? Surely Kane wanted them. Who wouldn't? Last night she'd seen how charmed he was by the youngsters' singing, and especially little Timmy.

She shook her head, remembering Timmy and Isaac's touching performance. Isaac, so childlike himself.

Not so with Kane. He was all man. *Mature* man!

Enough of this dillydallying; she had work to do.

She pulled her head back through the window and shrugged into her robe.

Bustling down the hall into the kitchen, her first chore was to stoke up the fire in the stove. Mentally she ticked off her picnic menu as she pulled items from the larder.

In short order she assembled the ingredients for a loaf of bread. While the kneaded dough was rising, she mixed up a batch of chocolate cookies, and then scones that she would serve with lemon curd. She boiled eggs to devil, arranged a bed of lettuce and chicory on a platter, and piled the center with corn marinated with onion juice, mustard, and French dressing, that she'd canned last spring; and surrounded it with slices of ham, pickled cucumbers, and tomatoes.

As the bread baked, she hurried back into her bedroom to change.

Already past ten. Kane would arrive in less than an hour.

Hastily she slipped into the dress she'd laid out the night before. The blue-flowered poplin, with the puffed sleeves and the fitted bodice with the little point that made her waist seem even tinier than tiny. Finally, she ran a brush through her tumble of curls.

She had yet to check in at the sheriff's office to give Spike instructions for the day. Rushing out the back door, she strode across her little garden to the adjacent building.

"Otis' wife picked him up early this morning," the deputy informed her when she entered.

"Good. That means we won't have to feed him lunch." She glanced at the calendar on the wall above her desk, relieved that in her zeal to be with Kane she had not forgotten any appointments. "Anything on the teletype about the antics of Butch Cassidy and the Sundance Kid?"

"Not this mornin'."

"You might take a look at Deacon's left rear shoe. Yesterday he seemed to be limping a bit."

"Will do."

"I'll be gone most of the afternoon, so you're in charge."

"No problem."

"I'll check in when I get back."

"Sheriff business?" His eyes glinted with amusement as he assessed her pretty dress and pointy shoes.

He might be slow, but he wasn't that slow.

Jane felt a flush creep up into her cheeks. "Half and half," she said stiffly. "Showing a newcomer Old Man Craig's place."

"That Kane Braxton fellow?"

"Where'd you get that idea?" She crossed her arms and glared at him.

"Met up with Zeke Pool when I was pickin' up the post. Said he rented the fella a buggy for the day. The one he saves fer weddin's and funerals."

"I thought Zeke didn't let anybody drive that buggy but himself."

"That's what Isaac said to him."

"Oh, Isaac was at the post office, too?"

Spike nodded. "Zeke said everybody's got his price. And since he'd be escortin' the sheriff. . ." He snickered. "I won't tell ya what Isaac said to that."

Jane's stomach clenched. Of all the nerve! She wasn't surprised at Spike and Zeke, but Isaac, of all people. She could just imagine how Henrietta's ears were flapping. "I'm surprised you boys didn't set up a poker table and bring out the chips. Invite the whole town to join the game."

"Why I couldn't do that, Miss Sheriff." Spike grinned. "I'm on duty."

"One would hardly know it," Jane muttered, picking up the pile of mail. She gave it a cursory glance and threw it back on her desk.

"I'll check on Deacon," Spike smirked, scuttling out before she could say anything more.

"You do that!"

It seemed her business belonged to the whole town. Even Isaac had gotten into the act. What happened to loyalty?

Fuming with indignation, Jane scurried back across the garden and stomped into her kitchen. Assaulted by the smell of the fresh baked bread, she hurried over to the oven and pulled out the loaf, which she felt like slamming onto the counter but held back. She didn't want it to fall. Especially since it looked just about perfect. Golden brown, with just the right amount of crustiness.

She sighed and dropped into the chair in front of the table, where she allowed herself a moment of dejection. But only a moment! As always, her sunny nature rescued her. She was not about to let this silly gossip ruin her day. No indeed.

She glanced at the round clock over the kitchen door and leaped to her feet, her tarnished enthusiasm renewed by her optimistic spirit and the fact that Kane Braxton would be there within minutes.

Hastily she assembled her picnic in the large wicker basket she'd lined with a red and white checkered cloth. In addition to what she'd prepared, she added a jar of pears she had canned with ginger and lemon slices last fall, and finally, along with the cooled loaf of bread, she tucked in matching napkins and utensils, along with two blue willow plates, a pitcher of homemade cider, and a pair of crystal goblets.

And just in time!

No sooner had she finished, than the front doorbell clanged.

He was here.

Her mouth went suddenly dry.

Why was she so nervous? Kane Braxton was the one pursuing her, not the other way around. He was the one who had suggested this excursion, not she.

The bell clanged again.

After all, she was the sheriff of Whispering Bluff. A responsible, qualified professional. She had been in tighter situations than this with hardened criminals. Not often, but on occasion. This should be as easy as shooting a tin can at twenty paces.

So why should this little romantic interlude feel more like trying to hit a flea at fifty paces?

The doorbell clanged for the third time.

Well, at least he wouldn't think her too eager.

She willed herself to composure. Then, she straightened, took a deep breath, strode across the kitchen, through the parlor, and yanked open the front door.

She had thought herself prepared. But oh, my!

Her heart leaped at the sight of him, standing in the threshold—surely the handsomest man this side of the Continental Divide.

Daylight did not diminish his elegant aspect, nor expose any flaws. Rather, it accentuated his manly perfection, his golden mane waving back from his smooth, tanned brow. His striking silver eyes that now gleamed down into hers.

"Good mornin', Miss Jane."

A thrill, sharp as an electric current, coursed through her veins, striking her momentarily mute.

"I was concerned you had run out on me. . .or had urgent sheriff business. Had you not answered the door when you did, I fear I would have left in despair." Kane's broad shoulders slumped, as if to prove the point.

Hyperbole in the extreme, to say nothing of the melodrama. All of which served to slap some sense back into Jane. But then she saw his playful grin and realized the intention of his teasing exaggeration.

"I am a woman of my word, Mr. Braxton," she said pertly. "Only the pursuit of the most nefarious criminal would have kept me from our engagement. And my deputy informed me just moments ago that Butch Cassidy and the Sundance Kid have not been sighted in these parts in the last twenty-four hours."

He laughed. "Well, that's certainly a relief. But if they were, at least I'd have the comfort of knowin' I'm bein' protected by the best little shot in three counties. . .or is it four?"

"Three," she smiled modestly, her confidence returning with each compliment. "Goodness, where are my manners?" She stepped back abruptly. "Won't you come in?"

"I thought you'd never ask." He grinned, a lopsided, flirting grin that sent her heart soaring once again as he stepped into her little parlor.

"Somethin' certainly smells mighty fine in here." He sniffed.

Jane gave him a bemused smile but said nothing. He'd find out soon enough.

He looked around. "Why this is charmin'," he said with a note of surprise. "Most charmin'!" His gaze lingered over the pink and yellow–flowered chintz chairs and the pink Victorian settee with the antimacassars Jane had tatted, the throw pillows depicting Colorado wildflowers she'd done in needlepoint, and the lace curtains she'd sewn on her new Singer sewing machine.

"I can see your fine handiwork everywhere. I'm most impressed."

"I'm glad you approve."

"Approve, dear lady, is hardly the word. I am enchanted— and you a sheriff. Why, I never expected—"

"Because I'm a sheriff?" Jane frowned. At first she'd felt a sense of pride, now, a surge of irritation.

Kane Braxton's first pop of imperfection!

"What makes you think, sir, that a sheriff can't—"

"Oh, please, dear lady," Kane interrupted, "don't mis-understand." He looked genuinely alarmed. "I meant it only as a compliment. That you should carry out the duties of a county sheriff, keepin' law and order, goin' on patrol, apprehendin' vicious criminals like Butch Cassidy and the Sundance Kid—and I might add without a flicker of fear in those beautiful blue eyes of yours—and yet still find time to do this lovely handiwork, sing in the choir, and be in charge of the potluck supper, and make those delicious chocolate cookies. . ." His hot gaze swept her whole person. "And I'd even be willin' to wager you sewed that pretty little outfit you're wearin'."

"Stop," Jane cried, mollified, beginning to laugh. "You've said quite enough."

"Believe me, Miss Jane—"

"I believe you."

But he would not be still. "What I'm tryin' to say is, it's clear your life is full and rich and not centered on just your important career, but you have other qualities and creative talents that occupy you. Which I'm sure comes as a relief to any man who might hold"—he paused, gazing down at his highly polished boots—"a relief to any man who might harbor. . .serious intentions."

There was a moment of awkward silence. Then Kane muttered gruffly, "I apologize if I've said too much."

Jane swallowed.

She cleared her throat.

"Not at all," she murmured. "Though I fear all these compliments may give me a swelled head."

"Never!" Kane assured her, reaching for her hand.

She allowed him to hold it for but a moment, then shyly pulled away. "I hope you'll think my culinary skills live up to my decorating ones."

"I suspect they will. Judging from that chocolate cookie last night." His smile was warm, making it quite difficult for Jane to unlock her gaze from his.

"Well, then," she said when she could manage, "let me just get my cloak and we'll be on our way."

She hurried down the hall to her bedroom and shut the door behind her. She leaned back against it and closed her eyes.

Kane Braxton was a very special man.

She was more convinced than ever that her womanly instinct had been right from the very beginning. Isaac, with his constant know-it-all doubts and concerns, had been wrong. Thankfully, she had paid no attention.

Why, Kane Braxton might very well be the man the good Lord had finally intended to step in and steal her heart.

She let out a prolonged sigh.

Yes, indeed, this could very well be one of the most important days of her life.

Slipping into her periwinkle cape, she peered into the vanity mirror and nibbled her lips to give them color. It was not necessary to pinch her cheeks; they were already pink with the flush of excitement, and her blue eyes sparkled bright with anticipation.

As she whirled back into the parlor, she enjoined, "I need a strong man to carry the picnic basket."

"At your service, milady." Kane bowed gallantly.

At the door of the kitchen he paused. He leaned against the jamb and crossed his arms, taking a moment to view the polished copper pots hanging above the stove, the artfully displayed blue willow plates on the sunny yellow wall, and the burnished wooden trestle table in the middle of the room.

"Will your talents never end, Miss Sheriff?" He shook his head. "You are truly a wonderment." As he picked up the picnic basket, he gave her a tender smile. "I foresee an exceptional day, Miss Jane. A truly exceptional day."

fourteen

At the top of the rise, just beyond where the schoolhouse once stood, Jane touched Kane's arm, urging him to stop the buggy. "See that land? That's Old Man Craig's place." She pointed north over the patchwork of fields, hazed with green sprouts, their furrows narrowing toward the horizon.

"That's quite a spread," Kane observed.

"One day, when I don't have to return to duty so soon, I'll take you to meet him. That is, if you're interested."

Kane contemplated the scene. "Yes, I think I would like to visit Old Man Craig." He smiled over at her. "Yes, my eyes are opening to many possibilities. . .the Craig farm among them."

Jane gave a nervous laugh and glanced away.

His hand lightly covered hers. "Ah, I've embarrassed you again." He chuckled. "Just as I intended."

Relieved by his levity, she looked up with a playful pout. "You're lucky you're not Isaac. I'd have given him a poke for that."

But since this was Kane, since. . . She melted in the warmth of his teasing smile.

Abruptly, he picked up the reins. "Speakin' of that boy Isaac, he seems to hold you in quite a special regard."

"He'd better! He's been my best friend since we were knee-high to grasshoppers."

"Friend?" Kane gave her a sidelong glance. "Only friend? It may appear that way to you, Miss Jane, but I suspect his feelin's for you run considerably deeper than that."

"Nonsense," she scoffed. "Does a person with serious intentions twist a girl's nose and tickle her ribs?"

Kane laughed. "If he's ten years old."

"He acts like it sometimes, I grant you. But Isaac's got

his serious side, too. And loyalty's his middle name." Jane shrugged. "Maybe that's why he gave you that impression last night, with all his shenanigans about being my protector." She smoothed her skirt over her knees. "I set him straight, though."

Kane glanced at her benignly. "That you didn't need a protector from me, or one in general?"

"Be serious!" She rolled her eyes and shook her curls in an effort to deflect his intuitive perception. "I assure you, Isaac's intentions toward me do not extend beyond nose twisting and rib tickling. Nor mine toward him."

"I'm relieved to hear that." His heated gaze was speculative. "I wouldn't want to move in on someone else's dreams."

Someone else's dreams? Isaac's dreams?

After a moment he turned, and giving the reins a snap, urged the mare forward.

If a response was called for, Jane was at a loss. She sucked in her cheeks and fastened her gaze on the road, locking her fingers in her lap. Her ears echoed with the *click-clack* of the wheels, the squeak of leather, as the little buggy bounced along the rutted road between the high Osage orange hedges toward Rikum's Pond.

As they rode through the small grove of cottonwoods, the air was rich with the scent of the damp earth. Watercress and fragile spring flowers nestled among the rocks surrounding Rikum's Pond, and willows dipped their languid branches into the stream that fed it, their tips pulled over the pebbles by the chortling waters.

Jane remembered the last time she'd come here. With Isaac. Just two days before the fire.

They'd come on horseback, not in a fancy buggy. She'd ridden Deacon and he'd borrowed Spike's old horse, Outlaw, a misnomer for one of the meekest horses in town.

It had been just such a day as this. Bright sun. Sweet-scented breeze. . .

But no fancy picnic! Just sandwiches they'd stuck in their saddlebags, berries stolen from the vines crowding the creek, and chocolate cookies she'd tucked in—or Isaac wouldn't have spoken to her. No special cider, just the cool, clear water from the creek feeding Rikum's Pond, and Isaac's teasing brown eyes laughing into hers.

No heart-pounding exhilaration as she felt now. No breathless anticipation. No lingering looks exchanged, filled with passion and promise.

⁊⁊

The shadows were long by the time the buggy drew up in front of Jane's cottage.

As Kane followed her into the kitchen, carrying the picnic basket with the remains of their lunch, she glanced at the clock. "My goodness, I had no idea it was so late."

"Does it matter?" he asked, putting the basket on the table.

"Only that I promised Spike—"

"I'm sure Spike will forgive you." Kane smiled, grasping her hands in his. He gazed thoughtfully down at them, then lifted his eyes. "It was a fine day, Miss Jane. One I will always remember."

"As will I, Kane, always," she murmured.

"I want you to know how much I admire your culinary skills and how appreciative I am of all the trouble you went to, to make it special."

"It was no trouble. I enjoyed every minute."

"But I must confess, dear Jane, even before this special day, you had won my heart."

She gave him a teasing smile. "You mean to say I didn't have to go to all my trouble?"

"Now you're toyin' with me, Miss Jane. I'm quite sincere." He gripped her hands more tightly, as if to ensure she wouldn't flee.

"I'm not gonna say it happened the first time I saw you. That would not be truthful. Though I did take notice, you standin' out there in front of your sheriff's office, that star glitterin' over your heart." He smiled fondly. "No, it was the second time! When I saw you dancin' through the woods like some spring sprite in your simple little blue frock and I had to rescue you from fallin' in the stream. I held your tiny little hands in mine just as I'm doin' now, and near drowned myself in those big blue eyes of yours, so guileless and good. It was at that very minute that you stole my heart."

Jane could hardly believe what she was hearing. Was it possible that this fine gentleman, this sophisticated man of the world, had the same desire for her, this simple little country girl, that she had for him? Of all the women he could have chosen?

If she were to believe the honeyed sweetness of his words and the sincerity in his eyes, it was true. Every fiber of her being tingled with the truth of it, every throb of her heart attested to it.

"Don't stop me, Miss Jane."

As if there were a chance.

"I need mightily to say what's on my mind and in my heart. When my sweet wife was taken from me. . ."

Were those tears glistening in his eyes?

He blinked and glanced away.

They were!

"Yes," he said, sighing. "We were so young."

"Oh, Kane," she whispered, restraining the impulse to gather him in her arms and comfort him.

He lifted his gaze. "That day that she died, in my arms, somethin' in me died, too." He swallowed. "I never thought I could have those feelin's for anyone else."

Jane saw the torment in his silver eyes as he struggled to speak. "And then, Miss Jane, I met you. . .and. . .and I dared to hope. May I be so bold as to say, knowin' you, my dear Miss Jane, I feel as if I've come alive again."

The earnestness of his smile brought such a tender response in her, such an agonizing empathy, she could only turn away, abashed by the intensity of it.

"Oh, I would despair if I thought I had caused you discomfort with my honesty," he said, his voice husky, registering his concern. "But I felt compelled to share what was in my heart in the hope that. . ."

Jane lifted her gaze. "Oh, Kane," was all she could manage. All she needed to manage, for in that moment, he silenced her lips with his.

She found herself melting in the power of his impassioned kiss, her senses springing to life with feelings she never knew existed.

❧

I probably shouldn't be doing this, Isaac thought, strolling down Main Street that same night after his supper. But he was curious. Danged if he wasn't.

As he passed the sheriff's office he saw Spike with his feet up on the desk. Probably readin' one of those racy dime novels like he did when Janie wasn't lookin'.

He pushed open the gate to her garden.

It always smelled good in Jane's garden: roses, lavender, night bloomin' jasmine. Even in winter, come to think of it, with the scent of pine from the tree near her back door. And most of the time warm smells comin' from her cheery little kitchen. Seemed like she almost always had somethin' temptin' bakin' in that oven of hers.

He knocked on the back screen door.

He could see through the kitchen into her pretty little parlor. Her curled up in that big chair next to the fireplace; a fire goin', the light dancin' around the room like little whirligigs.

Soon the weather would be too warm for a fire, but she'd keep one burnin' till it was. Said it made the room more cozy. Though he couldn't imagine a cozier room, especially with her little self in it.

"Who is it?" Jane called.

"Me. . .Isaac."

"Oh, you!" She didn't sound that happy about it. "Come in."

"You should keep the door locked," he said, striding into the parlor.

"Nobody locks their doors in Whispering Bluff," Jane

grumbled, looking up from her book.

"But you're the sheriff. You never know when some disgruntled felon might just get a hankerin' to get even." He plopped down into the chair opposite her, which had an indentation where his seat belonged, he'd been sittin' in it for so many years. Although she had changed the cover since he'd been gone to a pink and yellow flower pattern instead of the plaid that had covered it when her pa was alive.

Still, it wasn't so feminine that a fella didn't feel he could put up his feet, which he did, on the little footstool with the needlepoint cover she'd made to match.

"Livin' all alone like ya do, ya really should take more precautions."

"What are you, my protector?" Jane frowned. "Oh, yes, I forgot."

"You still mad at me?"

She gave him a disgusted look. "Stop putting on that woebegone expression. I'm not impressed. Yes, I'm mad at you. I'm mad at you for your shenanigans last night, and I'm mad at you for gossiping about me this morning."

"What d'you mean?"

"Don't try that innocent bit with me. Spike spilled the beans about you boys in a huddle at the post office."

"Strictly by chance," Isaac assured her. "I'd just gone in to pick up the mail."

"Uh-huh." She gave him a skeptical look.

"Honest. . .but I couldn't help overhearin'."

"And putting in your penny's worth."

"It cost that Kane fella a lot more than a penny to rent Zeke's buggy." Isaac leaned back and steepled his hands. "Was the price worth it?"

Jane slapped her book shut. "Isaac August, you are the most infuriating man—*boy*—I have ever met!"

She looked put out, all right, but there was a glow about her that told him it was not all that serious. Which made him suspect it was more than serious and he was gonna be real unhappy with her answer. Still, he wanted to know, bein' a glutton for punishment. "Well, was it?"

Jane glared at him for a moment longer, then couldn't contain herself. "Yes! If you must know." Lowering her gaze to the book in her lap, she added quietly, "Absolutely! The day was perfect!"

"I'm glad to hear it," Isaac managed, though his heart wasn't in it.

She looked up at him, her ire forgotten, her expression transformed. "Oh, Isaac, Kane's everything I imagined, even more than I'd hoped. You were so wrong about him. He is the kindest, most sensitive man."

She shook her head and smiled. "Why, you won't believe what he said when he thought you had feelings for me. Isn't that a laugh? You, of all people."

"Well, he's right," Isaac said staunchly. "Though I don't see what that has to do with anythin'."

"You know what I mean. *Special* feelings." Jane laughed.

Why was that so far-fetched? Of course he didn't. But still...

"I set him straight! Made it clear right off that our relationship was purely platonic—albeit soul mates," she added hastily when Isaac didn't seem all that amused about it.

"Anyway, he said he was glad, because he didn't want to move in on someone else's dream. Wasn't that the most sensitive thing you've ever heard?"

Fortunately, she didn't give Isaac a chance to answer.

He doubted he could have held his tongue. If he'd ever heard a slick line, that was it. So what if Janie *was* locked into Isaac's dreams? Not that she was. But if she were—

Not want to move in on somebody else's dreams. Ha!

The bounder was a real sweet talker, all right. And a snake, the way he wound his words around an unsuspecting girl's heart.

Oblivious to Isaac's sudden silence, Jane described the afternoon, her sentences tumbling over each other with breathless exuberance: how Kane had shown an interest in the Craig farm; the picnic; his extravagant compliments and conversation. . .

Isaac watched her savor every detail—even though when she hesitated he knew she was leaving parts out—reliving it all with such joyous enthusiasm he had not the nerve to interrupt her. Though in his estimation, her banter had gotten more improbable by the minute.

Couldn't she see that?

"I said I wanted lots and lots of children," she said. "Me being an only child myself, with my mama dying before I could even know her, and wishing I had sisters and brothers—thank goodness for you." She gave Isaac's hand a perfunctory pat.

"What did he say to that?"

"He said he certainly could understand, and I'd need a big house for all those youngsters. And I described the kind of house I'd dreamed of—actually, I described Jacob Hostetler's farmhouse, but with a few more rooms. And Kane said I'd need lots of help to take care of such a big house and passel of young 'uns, so I'd probably have to marry a rich man."

"Very astute," Isaac muttered under his breath.

Did he have anyone in mind?

"I told him that the man I married didn't have to be rich in money but he did have to be rich in the love of God, because that was the most important thing in a home and a family."

"And what did Mr. Perfect say to all that?"

"I will ignore your sarcasm." She gave him a withering look. "Contrary to what you might believe, Isaac, Kane and I have a great deal in common. You'd be surprised."

I would, indeed.

She lowered her head, gazing absently at the book in her lap. "When I got up this morning I knew this was going to be a special day, and it was. I made up my mind I was going to learn all about him, his hopes, his dreams. . . . And I did."

Isaac frowned. He couldn't hold his peace any longer. "What were they, Janie? What were Kane Braxton's hopes and dreams? I haven't heard a word about his hopes and dreams, only what you told him about yours. From what I can tell, he knows all about you, but you still know very little about him."

"How can you say that?" Jane stiffened. "Why—why. . ." Her eyes flashed. "You can't even begin to imagine. . . . Don't you believe me? Do I need to get it in writing to satisfy you?"

"I'm not the one he has to satisfy, Janie."

"Don't Janie me," she spat. "Why, Kane agreed with everything I said. What are you trying to do? Ruin something that was beautiful? It was as if—as if we were. . ." She thrust out her chin. "All right! It was as if Kane and I were soul mates!"

Isaac stared at her. "I thought it was you and me who were soul mates, Janie," he said quietly.

"I thought we were, too." Her eyes were hooded and hurt, her lips tight. "Once! Now I'm not so sure, the way you're acting."

They sat in silence, Isaac gazing at Jane's bowed head, Jane studying her clasped hands.

When she finally spoke again, her voice was low. "I can't believe this. I just can't believe it. You've always wanted what was best for me. And now this fine man comes into my life, and I think—I believe, that I've finally found my true love, and you want to ruin everything." She looked up at him with miserable eyes. "Why, if I didn't know you better, I'd think Kane was right about you. You're acting like a jealous person."

"Jealous? Me?" Isaac leaped to his feet. "So I can't be honest with you anymore, Jane?" He glowered down at her. "I can't express honest concerns without you accusin' me of bein' jealous?" He turned and strode toward the door. "Well, if that's the way it's goin' to be from now on, Miss Sheriff Jane McKee, that's fine with me! It's your bed to lie in. Obviously, you don't want me givin' you advice. Even if you *could* use it!"

He couldn't resist the last jab!

fifteen

Isaac slammed the screen door behind him and stalked down Jane's garden path. He yanked open the gate with such force, it came close to ripping from its hinges. But as he strode up Main Street, his pace slowed the closer he got to the saloon. By the time he had stomped up the back stairs to his ma's apartment, he felt as low as the belly of a lizard sprawlin' on a rock.

He'd done it again! He'd infuriated his best friend! Real serious this time! And this time he reckoned she wouldn't be as quick to forgive.

"I know I shouldn't have opened my big mouth, Ma," he said, throwing himself down on the striped-cushioned pine chair in his mother's tiny kitchen. "But I just couldn't help myself. Janie's so gullible, she believes everything that sweet talker tells her." Crossing his arms on the table, he cocked an elbow and rested his chin on his fist, glowering at his mother as if she had something to do with it.

Jackie Lee pulled a couple of mugs from the cupboard above the sink. "Made some hot chocolate. Maybe a cup would bring you some comfort. With a fluffy homemade marshmallow floating in it."

"No marshmallow."

"You used to love marshmallows when you were a young'un."

"I'm not a young'un anymore."

"Even though you act like one?" She slid the steaming cup across the table.

He dropped his arm. "What's that supposed to mean?"

"I wasn't there." She shrugged. "You tell me."

"All I did was tell Janie what I thought. Like I always do. This time she got all huffed up and insulted."

"You mean you weren't your usual tactful self?"

He gave his mother a shamefaced look. "Apparently she didn't think so. Anyway, she claims she's found her true love—her *true love*! Can you beat that? In a week she finds her true love, and she says I'm ruinin' everything 'cause I'm suspicious." He shook his head. "I just don't want to see her hurt again, Ma."

"Her true love being that Kane Braxton fellow everybody's talking about?"

Isaac nodded morosely, fiddling with the handle of his mug.

Jackie Lee blew the steam off the top of her chocolate. "What's he done to make you think he'll break her heart?"

"Nothin'!" Isaac shook his head. "In fact just the opposite. He's sayin' all the right things, doin' all the right things. He's *too* perfect. What does a rich city slicker like him, with his elegant clothes and fine manners and his smooth talk, see in a sweet little country girl like my Janie?"

"*Your* Janie?" His mother arched a brow.

"You know what I mean, Ma." He began to squirm under her sudden scrutiny. "Ah, not you, too! First that Kane fella tells Janie I have designs on her, then she accuses me of soundin' jealous, and now I'm gettin' the *look* from my own ma." He crossed his arms and glared at her. "It isn't like that between me and Janie."

"Mmm." His mother lifted her cup, blew delicately against the steam again, and took a dainty sip.

"It isn't! And you know it. It never has been."

"You'd know that better than I." She lifted the corner of her apron and gently tapped her lips. "If I can give you a woman's perspective, son, hearing compliments and sweet words whispered into her ear and feeling cherished and admired, counts a lot with a girl."

"Janie doesn't need all that silly stuff. She knows she's admired. Everybody admires her, or else why would she be elected sheriff?"

Isaac saw his mother come just short of rolling her eyes. As if she thought he was some dimwit. Her words confirmed it.

"For a smart boy, you're really. . .*really* not so smart. I've been trying to explain to you that Kane Braxton is telling Janie what she needs to hear. That she's lovely and cherished and adored. And why shouldn't he tell her that? It's the truth. And it makes her happy." She looked at Isaac sternly. "And who are you to say the man doesn't mean it? If you think Janie's so fine, why wouldn't he think so?"

"Okay! So you made your point." Isaac scowled. "But what if I'm right and he *is* just danglin' her along for his own pleasure, and he *does* break her heart?"

"Then you'll be the good friend she needs, waiting in the wings." His mother shook her head impatiently.

"That goes without sayin'." Absently, Isaac reached for his mug and took a big gulp. "That's hot!" he shrieked, sticking out his tongue and fanning it with his hand.

His mother tossed him a sympathetic smile and continued stirring her own chocolate to cool it.

"You know," she murmured thoughtfully, "it occurs to me that maybe you're a bit impulsive. Like with that hot chocolate. You take a big gulp before testing it out."

She tapped the spoon on the rim of the mug. "Sometimes it's prudent to wait, let things cool down. See what transpires before jumping in with your grand opinion and making everybody mad at you."

"Gee, Ma, you really know how to make a fella feel better." But he realized she wasn't finished.

"Start trusting in God's plan, Isaac, instead of your own. He works things out. Give Him time. Exercise a little patience. Don't you know, the Bible praises patience. It's a fruit of the spirit. 'We know that all things work together for good to them that love God, to them who are the called according to his purpose.' Think of it this way, Isaac: Janie's purpose is God's problem, not yours. It'll ease your mind a whole lot."

"Your Bible quotes always ease my mind, Ma." He didn't hold back. He *did* roll his eyes.

"It wouldn't hurt you to get a bit more familiar." His mother sighed. "The Bible sure has been a comfort in my times of trouble."

Ma was an authority on trouble, for certain.

Jackie Lee dropped her hands into her lap. "Now, one last bit of advice."

"More? I don't know if I can take in any more."

She cleared her throat. "My final advice to you is to swallow that pride of yours and mend those bridges first thing tomorrow. Your friendship with sweet Janie runs too long and too deep to let this go on. The longer things fester the harder they are to fix."

Now that was somethin' about which Ma was an authority!

Isaac took a more prudent sip of his hot chocolate and gazed fondly at her. "Speakin' of pride, and things festerin'. . . At the risk of havin' both the women in my life down on me, you might think about takin' your own advice, Ma. If I may be so bold. You might start thinkin' about the pride you've been chokin' on for years."

His mother's expression suddenly darkened. "I guess my little homily on minding one's business didn't come through very well."

"It's about time somebody spoke up to you, Ma. Big Jim's gotta be pretty weary of waitin' around for you to see the light."

His mother started to protest, but Isaac put up a restraining hand. "He loves you, Ma. He's never made any secret of it, and I know you love him. I've seen your face when he looks at you. And I've heard your tears. You're just too ashamed and prideful to admit it." He took a deep breath. "It seems to me it's about time you swallowed that pridefulness in your own soul that's been—how did you put it—festerin' all these years. You deserve to be happy, Ma, and so does he."

Jackie Lee lifted her chin. "You mend your bridges. I'll mend mine. And in my own time." But he sensed a tinge of doubt behind her sullen stare, and then she dropped her gaze.

"Ya can't teach, Ma, if ya can't learn," he said gently. " 'A man's pride shall bring him low: but honour shall uphold the humble in spirit.' That goes for ladies, too."

His mother's head shot up. "And where did that bit of wisdom come from?"

"Thought you'd recognize it." Isaac grinned. "Learned it in Sunday school in the fifth grade. Becca's ma, Faith, made us memorize the Proverbs when we talked outta turn."

A small smile played around his mother's lips. "And with that mouth of yours, I reckon you learned most of them."

❧

Jane had jumped at the sound of the screen door slamming.

She couldn't believe it. They'd had their tiffs before, she and Isaac, but never like this. Never where one of them just stomped out.

She might have thought it was the four years he'd been gone that had changed him. She remembered how worried she'd been about that, and how relieved that he'd come home with his playful, loving spirit intact—and how things had fallen into place just as they'd always been.

Until now!

She wanted to be furious with him.

But it was so out of character.

She frowned, staring into the fire.

When Kane entered the picture, everything suddenly seemed to change between Isaac and her.

Isaac had certainly made no secret of his opinion of the man. . .and his doubts about him. And then tonight when he'd shown up just so he could quiz her about the day and criticize. And then, when she'd suggested that he sounded jealous—out of the blue he'd exploded.

It wasn't like him at all. He was usually so good-natured and easy about things, even when he was irritated with her. He'd just let it pass.

No, not like him at all.

She rested her elbow on the arm of her chair and rested her forehead in her hand, gazing absently at the book in her lap.

Was it possible that he actually *was* jealous? That Kane had seen what she had missed? What maybe even Isaac himself didn't realize? That Isaac *did* have special feelings for her?

Oh dear, no!

Oh, she hoped she was wrong.

With all her heart she prayed it wasn't so.

She knew too well the pain of unrequited love. And if, indeed, Isaac did care for her in that special way, unrequited love was all that it could ever be. Because every time she even thought of Kane Braxton, she was surer and surer that he was the man she'd been waiting for.

That's why, when Isaac showed up the next morning, Jane wasn't sure she was ready to welcome him. After all, he had caused her a sleepless night.

But seeing him standing on her back steps, with his crooked, contrite grin, and his thatch of nutmeg hair springing around his endearing, ruddy face, she couldn't suppress a smile. . .or her relief.

"I just made coffee. Want a cup?" She pulled open the screen door.

"Why else do ya think I'm here? I was passin' by, and this rich aroma wafted out, and I thought, I'll bet Janie'd share a cup a that fine-smellin' brew. Even with a sinner like me."

"Come on in, you dolt." She shook her head. "You're so full of—"

"Don't say it."

"Nonsense."

"I really came ta tell ya I'm sorry, Janie." He stood by the kitchen table, twisting the brim of his hat between his fingers. "I had no business actin' the way I did last—"

"You don't need to say any more. Anyway, you're forgiven." She smiled up into his endearing, freckled face. "I'm sorry, too."

"What are you sorry about?"

"I don't know." She giggled, a feeling of warmth and affection coming over her. "Just in case."

She pushed him down into one of the ladder-back chairs. "You sit there and keep out of trouble while I pour the coffee."

Isaac slapped his two palms on the table. "Any a yer scones floatin' around?"

"You're shameless."

"With strawberry jam?"

Jane gave him a beleaguered look. But her heart was light. It appeared things were back to normal.

At least for the time being!

sixteen

By the middle of June, Whispering Bluff was already in a flurry of preparation for the Fourth of July celebration. It was the main topic of conversation at the barbershop and most certainly, Jane knew firsthand, at the post office.

She had been there when Eunice Figg prevailed on Mavis to make "His Honor the mayor's" George Washington costume. "Being such a fine seamstress, you are the only one I would trust. As you know"—Eunice sniffed importantly, the plumage on her blue bonnet bouncing—"His Honor's reading of the Declaration of Independence will be the highlight of the ceremony, and it's vitally important that his outfit be perfect."

"I'd be happy to," Mavis murmured. Even though Jane knew she had already volunteered to sew all the costumes for the children's tableau.

"I'll help you," she whispered.

The klatch of Henrietta's ten o'clock regulars: the mayor's wife, Bertha Warner, Lilly Johnson, and Naomi Pool were clustered around in front of the counter, behind which the postmistress was sorting mail.

Jane had come to refer to them—but only to Isaac—as the gossip mavens.

She glanced at the clock on the wall above the wanted posters. She should have known better than to come at this hour—but she'd been so anxious to see if the material for her Fourth of July outfit had arrived.

Eunice sighed. "Thank you so much, Mavis dear. I'm just beside myself with all my responsibilities." She shook her head, rolling her eyes heavenward, as if the burdens of the world hung on her bony shoulders. "But you know me; I just can't say no."

"I can't imagine what this community would do without you, Eunice," Naomi boomed, her husky voice obsequious even as it grated.

Jane knew Naomi was courting Eunice for a coveted membership in the Garden Club.

"Here you design the Garden Club float and you can't even ride in it," Lilly murmured.

"Why is that, Eunice?" asked Sarah Mortinson, who had been idly reading the wanted posters.

"She's the only local Daughter of the American Revolution," Bertha said. "There's nobody but her to represent them."

"It's my patriotic duty." Eunice sighed. "You know I'd much rather be riding with you girls."

Jane had heard enough of this nonsense. "Any mail for me, Henrietta?" she asked pleasantly.

The postmistress reached into a bin by the mail slots and handed her a mailing cylinder. "Wanted posters." She also pulled out a letter and tossed it on the counter. "Form letter from the U.S. Marshal's office. And. . ." She reached for a package from the table behind her. "The material for your Fourth of July outfit."

"Did you check the color?" Jane winked at Mavis.

"Don't be a smarty, Miss Sheriff."

Mavis turned to Bertha Warner. "The barbershop competition should be interesting. The Harmonizers might get a run for their money this year."

Bertha's chins quivered. "Where did you get that idea? Doc says the Harmonizers are sounding better than ever! They've won for the last three years. I don't see why that will change."

"And you should know, Bertha, Doc being lead singer." Naomi threw a hefty arm around the buxom woman's shoulders. Bertha was also a member of the Garden Club.

"I've heard good things about John Aubrey's group," Sarah interjected. "With Isaac August the lead singer, and almost a professional. Could be an exciting competition."

"Experience counts," Bertha snapped. "The Harmonizers

will win again, hands down. You wait and see!"

"I've forgotten what John's group call themselves," Mavis said. "The Metronomes?"

"Monotones." Jane smiled. "Because their harmony is so close."

"They should be called the Upstarts," Bertha muttered, "they're so cocky,"

"They're not cocky, Bertha, they're just confident," Mavis responded mildly. "There's a difference."

"No, they're cocky." Jane laughed, turning to leave. "That's part of the fun!"

At that moment the post office door swung open, and Kane Braxton strode in. He stopped abruptly when he saw Jane, his face breaking into what could only be described—even by the most objective observer—as a dazzling smile. "Why, Miss Sheriff, what a happy surprise." He doffed his gray Stetson. "Good morning."

Would she always react this way when she saw the man? Would her body grow hot and tingly? Would her palms grow moist? Would her heart flutter in her bosom like the wings of a caged bird?

Would a mere "Good morning" always make her melt?

Oh, she truly hoped so.

As sheriff, Jane had preferred to keep her feelings for Kane discreet. But obviously, Kane felt no such constraint. His expression conveyed more than just a passing interest as he allowed his silver gaze to caress her in a way that held such warmth and familiarity that she trembled under its incandescence.

"Good morning to you, Mr. Braxton," she managed, suddenly aware that the gossips had quieted behind her and were watching with crackling curiosity.

Kane finally raised his eyes and noticed Mavis standing beside Jane. . .then the gawking quartet at the counter. "Good morning, ladies."

A medley of murmured "Good mornings" greeted him: Eunice Figg's sniffing contralto, Naomi's husky bass, Bertha Warner's reluctant alto. Only Lilly Johnson's whispery soprano remained mute, her mouth slightly agape, her eyes unusually bright.

Apparently oblivious to the stir he had created, Kane drew a thin envelope from his inner coat pocket and pushed it across the counter to Henrietta.

Even the dour postmistress was momentarily affected by his smile. And why not; the air in the little post office seemed charged by Kane Braxton's electric presence.

"Why, Janie," Mavis whispered, giving her sleeve a surreptitious tweak, "you're blushing."

Jane glared at her friend.

The postmistress scanned Kane's letter. "Mmm, Bank of New York. It won't go out until late tomorrow. I hope that's all right."

Jane had never seen the woman so solicitous.

"That will be fine, Miss Pryce." He dropped coins for postage on the counter.

"We were just talking about the Fourth of July, Mr. Braxton," Eunice Figg sniffed, tapping her right nostril with a lace hankie. "I do hope you plan to ride in the parade."

He glanced up. "To be honest, Mrs. Figg, I hadn't given it much thought."

"But, Mr. Braxton, you have such a fine horse." Lilly Johnson had found her voice, breathy and fawning.

"Well thank you, Miss Lilly. But from what I've been hearin' there's more folks in the parade than to watch. I doubt my participation would be much missed."

"That's not so. You would be missed." Lilly turned to Jane. "You convince him, Jane."

Jane studied the planks of the worn pine floor, not trusting herself to meet Kane's gaze. "I'm sure Mr. Braxton can make up his own mind about such things."

"Jane is leading the parade, you know," Mavis said.

"But only because I'm sheriff," she assured him modestly, finally lifting her eyes. "The sheriff always leads the Fourth of July parade."

He gave her a fond smile. "I can think of no more fittin' person than you, Miss Janie." The way he caressed her name, drew out each letter with such tenderness, it would have been nigh on impossible for anyone present to miss his meaning.

"And she's carrying the flag," Mavis added.

"Well then," Kane said, "that settles it."

"Then you *will* ride in the parade," chirped Lilly, clapping her hands.

"On the contrary. If Miss Jane is leading the parade, I want to be watchin' and cheerin' her on."

"Oh." Lilly collapsed like a deflated doll.

Oh dear. Jane's heart sank. There was no doubt now that the disappointed Lilly, and the rest of the gossip squad, would have no qualms about blowing this little exchange completely out of proportion. The word of Kane's obvious interest would spread with the fervor of a wind-whipped prairie fire.

❧

In the last month, three evenings out of the week, Jane had been distracted by the pulsing beat of Hitch Chapell's drums echoing from the church basement across the street, as the disparate little ragtag marching band rehearsed. It was a miracle how they managed to pull it together every year, but somehow they always did. Albeit with more spirit than skill!

The choir was also having additional rehearsals, preparing a medley of patriotic anthems for the ceremony after the parade. Included was a heart-stirring rendition of "The Battle Hymn of the Republic" Isaac had arranged especially for the occasion.

It was at practice the week before the performance that John Aubrey, looking mighty worried, hurried up to Isaac and Big Jim.

Jane, standing nearby, heard him tell them that Cliff Walker had come down with serious laryngitis, and Doc Warner said he had to rest his vocal chords for at least two weeks. "Which means Cliff won't be able to sing with us."

Isaac's eyes narrowed. "Do ya suppose the old reprobate's diagnosis had anything to do with his not wantin' us to be in the competition fer fear the Harmonizers might lose?"

"Doc ain't that kind of a fellow," Big Jim admonished.

"You're sure about that?" Isaac frowned, obviously not wholly convinced. Then he shrugged. "Maybe he's not. But that doesn't alter the situation. How are we gonna get a replacement on such short notice?"

John turned to Big Jim, desperation in his voice. "What about you, Jim?"

Big Jim laughed. "You don't need another bass, son. You already got Spike. What ya need is a good baritone—"

"Who's a quick learner, got a good sense of rhythm, knows how to harmonize. . ." Isaac shook his head, a woebegone look dragging down his usually cheery expression. "Fat chance!"

Jane hesitated. But only for a second! So what if Isaac didn't cotton to her idea. He wasn't coming up with a better solution.

She sidled up beside him. "What about Kane? He's a baritone."

With Jane's encouragement Kane had joined the choir two weeks before—causing a stir, especially among the single sopranos.

As it had turned out, he had a voice as rich and handsome as the man himself. So fine, in fact, that last Sunday Pru had given him the solo in " 'Are Ye Able,' Said the Master," with the choir coming in on the chorus. Everyone who attended services that morning agreed he had given an inspired performance.

The three men looked toward the row of chairs where Kane was holding court.

Kane surrounded by ladies was so commonplace, Jane had gotten past letting it bother her. In fact, it gave her a tad of pride.

He was hers! In the weeks since their picnic he hadn't missed a chance to make that clear. The post office being a prime example.

"Not a bad idea," John said.

Big Jim nodded. "Might just be the ticket."

Isaac's expression soured. "He'll look purty, anyway," he muttered.

"I'm going to ask him," John said. He glanced at the other two. "With your permission."

"Ya don't need my permission," Big Jim said. "And Spike ain't here to disagree."

Isaac didn't answer at first. Then he shrugged. "I suppose. Seein' as we're so desperate."

Jane was just about to give a sharp retort when he threw her a goodwill wink.

Well, at last it looked as if he was beginning to see the light.

"One thing for sure," Isaac muttered, "he'll get us the female vote."

Was that supposed to make her feel good?

She gave him a second look.

But his smile was benign.

seventeen

Jane knew it was partly for her sake that Isaac hadn't put up more of a fuss about agreeing to include Kane in his barbershop quartet.

"It's amazing, really, how it's turned out," she confided to Mary Aubrey one afternoon when she'd stopped by on her way back from making her rounds. "One day Isaac has hardly anything good to say about Kane, and the next they're thicker than thieves."

She was cuddling Mary's two-year-old, Nancy, on her lap as they sat on Mary's back steps watching Timmy throw a stick for his dog, Max.

"Why, Isaac even took Kane fishing. I thought he at least could have invited me to go along. Just the week before, he'd promised to take me. But he said, no, this trip was men only. Out of spite, I suppose, because I wouldn't go with him when he wanted me to."

She gave a mocking pout that quickly broke into a smile. "To be honest, I couldn't be happier. And relieved." She sighed. "It looks as if they're really becoming friends."

Mary, on the step beside her, returned her smile. "Your two main men."

"I guess you could say that." She rested her chin thoughtfully on the top of Nancy's soft, dark curls.

"I hardly see either of them lately, they're so busy practicing for the barbershop competition."

Now that the whole town knew that Kane was sweet on her, thanks to the gossip mavens, Jane felt comfortable in talking about it with her good friend.

"They're both so competitive. If they had nothing else in common, they'd have that. They're determined to beat Doc

108

Warner's Harmonizers. I think Isaac is still suspicious of Doc's diagnosis of Cliff Walker's laryngitis. I wouldn't admit this to anybody but you, Mary, but it would thrill me to pieces if the Monotones won. If only to see Bertha Warner eat crow. She acts so superior and positive that Doc's group can't be defeated."

Mary laughed. "I'm in the Garden Club with her. Bertha acts superior and positive about everything."

"Even more than Mrs. 'His Honor the mayor'?" Jane giggled.

"At least Eunice is a hard worker," Mary said. "In fact, she does more than her share. . .sometimes more than you want her to do." She brushed a curl from her toddler's cheek and smiled. "But that can be forgiven. Bertha's another matter. She just sits around criticizing and complaining."

"I know what you mean." Suddenly Jane gave a guilty laugh. "Listen to us. We're sounding like the town gossips. We'd better watch out. What does it say in Proverbs? 'The words of a talebearer are as wounds, and they go down into the innermost parts of the belly.'"

Mary laughed. "Aha. So that accounts for my indigestion." A chagrined expression swept across her sweet face. "You're right. Shame on us!"

They sat quietly for a time, basking in the warm sun and contemplating the damage loose tongues can do.

Absently, Jane mused, "Isaac's even hauling Kane around the countryside to look at property—like Isaac was some kind of land agent." She shook her head. "Amazing transformation. Such sudden devotion! God has really worked His wonders."

"Or Isaac has ulterior motives."

"What kind of ulterior motives would he have?"

Mary shrugged.

"I don't think so," Jane responded, dismissing the possibility. Nancy had begun to fret.

"I think she wants her mama," Jane said, handing her back to Mary.

"I think she wants a cookie." Mary reached into the pocket of her apron.

"Cookie," Nancy agreed, snatching it.

"Mind your manners." Mary frowned. "And eat it like a lady."

"A two-year-old lady." Jane smiled.

Someday I'll have a sweet, fat, little baby girl like Nancy.

"They're never too young to learn," Mary replied.

The two continued to sit in companionable silence, enjoying the perfume of petunias in full bloom by Mary's back door, listening to the Steller's jays quibbling in the oak, as they watched the little girl chomp on her treat and Timmy chase after his dog, the warm afternoon sun sending them into a contented reverie.

Mary wiped a crumb from Nancy's mouth with the corner of her apron. "Have you noticed lately how Isaac seems to have his eye on Betty Jean?"

"I think it's the other way around." Although Jane could see how Mary would get that idea, the way he was flaunting his attention on the girl. It was really a bit much, how he hung over her at choir, jumping up and getting her a glass of water, even when she didn't ask for one. Though Jane was relieved that Isaac had taken her suggestion about Betty Jean, she was getting pretty tired of the smug glances he was sending her every time he fawned over the girl.

Betty Jean wasn't the soul mate sort Jane might have chosen for her best friend, and she didn't personally have much in common with Betty Jean. But the girl was pretty—in a simple sort of way—and she was kind, and probably as good as any young woman in Whispering Bluff, and better than many.

Though she appeared a bit frivolous, with her big blinking brown eyes and perpetually adoring expression. But men seemed to like that kind of thing.

Jane could overlook her imperfections, though, because it was obvious Betty Jean was smitten with Isaac and admired his talent, always encouraging him to play his guitar and sing. . . even when it wasn't appropriate.

And she laughed at his jokes. A bit too loudly, it seemed

to Jane, making her suspicious that half the time Betty Jean didn't get them. But then, Jane had always found Betty Jean's sense of humor a bit lacking.

Oh, well, one couldn't expect everything.

Except in the case of Kane.

She sighed. He was one amazing human being!

"Betty Jean says he's very romantic," Mary said, breaking into her musings.

"Oh yes. . . . Oh, Isaac! Really?"

Mary laughed. "Who did you think I meant? As if I didn't know." She tweaked Nancy's cheek. "Yes, Isaac. I'll bet he is, too. With that fine voice of his, I can just imagine him in the moonlight, strumming his guitar and singing one of those love songs he writes."

"Love songs?" Jane cocked her head. "I never thought of his songs quite like that. More like plaintive cowboy laments. . . about broken hearts and missed opportunities. But I suppose they could be considered love songs."

"Makes you wonder what heartache he suffered in New York, doesn't it?" Mary said.

"No more than here," Jane murmured, "with him being the saloonkeeper's son."

"But here, he had you."

"That's so. And Peter and Becca. We used to call ourselves the Four Musketeers. But hardly the inspiration for love songs." Jane made a face. "Trust me. He doesn't have a romantic bone in his body."

Romantic? Isaac? Ridiculous! Jane had certainly never seen him that way. But now that Mary pointed it out, maybe it did take a bit of a romantic nature to write the kind of songs he did.

Obviously, Betty Jean Gordon had recognized that side of Isaac, judging from the blind adoration in her eyes when she looked at him.

"Well, I guess that explains it," Jane murmured.

"Explains what?"

"Why he's been helping himself to the flowers in my garden."

"He's giving flowers to Betty Jean?"

And all the time I'd just supposed they were for his mama.

❧

The Fourth of July finally arrived, and it couldn't have been a more perfect day for the parade: bright sun, cloudless sky, and a breeze with enough spirit to make the streamers dance and the flags show their colors.

Deacon tossed his head, causing the ribbons in his black mane to flutter. When he pawed the earth with nervous impatience, Jane leaned forward, giving a calming pat to the neck of her sleek bay stallion.

She straightened, adjusted the holster at her belt, and smoothed down the vest of her new white suede outfit. She'd sewn the blue and red buttons on just that morning, and last night finished the placket in the waist of the split, fringed skirt. It was all that hand-stitching on the jacket that had taken so much time.

All around her, folks were attired in their own patriotic finery: their horses plumed; manes and tails braided with the colors of the flag; buggies and wagons decorated with red, white, and blue crepe paper streamers and flowers. It was as grand a Fourth of July parade as Whispering Bluff had ever seen.

And she should know; she'd been riding in the parade for as long as she could remember, sitting tall and proud on her little pony, beside her papa, the sheriff.

Her hand rested lightly on the pole of the American flag, balancing in a holder attached to her saddle. A gentle wind sprang up, lifting its fringed corner.

For a moment, a poignant sadness swept over her. It was almost as if Papa were there, saying he was proud of her, and reminding her that he would always be riding by her side.

Accompanied by the little band's cacophony of discord, the mayor, resplendent as George Washington, powdered wig and all, ran about shouting warnings at the heedless boys racing their hoops and bicycles between the prancing horses, wagons, and buggies gathered in the field.

Finally, in a blast of ruffles and flourishes, the frazzled man hopped into a wagon packed tightly with the city's dignitaries, and lifted his megaphone. "Let the parade begin."

Jane adjusted her boots in the stirrups and straightened the brim of her white Stetson. She took a deep breath, snapped the reins, and Deacon pranced forward as the band struck the first notes of a spirited—if uneven—"Stars and Stripes Forever."

Main Street was lined with folks from all over the county who had gathered for the celebration, waving their flags and shouting. Children ran in and out among the crowd; toddlers perched on their daddy's shoulders, all the better to see; and old folks sat on stools along the dusty route. Weaving among them all, the Apple twins on stilts, a pair of identical Uncle Sams, distributed the cinnamon suckers that Luke Thompson always donated.

All the way down the parade route Jane searched for Kane. Smiling, waving from side to side, her gaze darted anxiously among the smiling faces, scanning the crowd for that one figure that would stand erect and tall above the rest.

It wasn't until she had reached the post office that she spotted him standing in front of Good Shepherd Community Church at the foot of Main Street. The sun seemed to beam just on him. The street, the town, the trees, the people gathered there, melted into the light of his gallant bearing. His pale blond hair a halo of gold in the sunlight.

She could feel her thudding heart race ahead of Deacon's prancing feet. Consciously, she pulled back, reining in her heart and her strutting stallion to a measured pace as she continued to smile and wave while every fiber of her being was drawn to Kane, standing with easy grace, his feet apart, his hands clasping his dove-gray Stetson.

As she drew closer, she saw Isaac leaning against the hitching rail just behind him.

Isaac, his dusty cowboy hat pushed to the back of his head, his chestnut hair springing in unruly waves around his ruddy brow, a proud grin lighting his endearing features.

She smiled back.

She always had to smile when she looked at Isaac.

What a study in contrasts: Kane so tall and elegant, formal in his bearing; and Isaac, dear Isaac, broad and sturdy—what else was there to say?

He was just. . .Isaac.

eighteen

Kane watched her as she rode toward him, the American flag fluttering beside her. A little angel in white, astride her sleek bay stallion.

His little angel in white!

It was in his power to make it so. All he had to do was say the word and she would be his. He knew that. He saw it in the way she leaned toward him, the light in her eyes when she looked at him.

Oh, yes, it was in his power to make her his.

If he chose to do so.

As she rode toward him down that dusty street he took it all in: the little town; the prairie; the purple hills beyond. He felt the fresh breeze against his face, the scent of summer flowers in his nostrils. Like the little angel in white, riding toward him, it was all his for the taking.

She reined to a stop in front of him.

He reached up to help her dismount.

Light as a feather, his little angel.

She gazed up at him with eyes bluer than the bluest sky, filled with hope and longing and trust.

A naked trust that no man could ever deserve. Least of all him!

A chord of longing twisted around his heart. Was love still possible for this derelict heart of his?

Everything in this town was warm and simple. Hopeful! Trusting.

Yes, this was his choice. It was his big chance.

Maybe his last!

This was the place that could serve his purpose, fulfill his dreams. And his sweet angel could help him make them all come true.

nineteen

Isaac looked over at the man standing to his right. Elegant! There was no other way to describe him.

For Janie's sake, he'd done his best to become the fella's best friend. But doggone, it just wasn't taking! There was still somethin' about the man that didn't smell right.

For one thing, even after all the time they'd spent together, he knew little more about Kane Braxton than the day they'd met. Kane played his past real close to the vest, and no amount of twistin' and turnin' on Isaac's part seemed to get a straight answer.

Except of course—and that was a big *except*—the afternoon when he and Kane went lookin' at property and Kane made a show about havin' to put some papers in his safe deposit box.

Just arrived from his New York bank, he'd said.

Implyin' they were documents too valuable to leave just lyin' around.

Such an important fella, he had to have two bank accounts? Maybe more, for all Isaac knew.

Isaac would have been satisfied with just one.

While Kane was otherwise occupied with Mr. Norwood at the bank, Isaac had taken a peek at the return address on the envelope. And there it was: The Bank of New York.

He hadn't decided yet whether or not to make use of the information. Send a letter, inquire after "Mr. Elegance." Somehow the thought of doing so made him feel disloyal to Janie. Maybe because he felt as if he would be doin' somethin' behind her back.

Maybe because he was afraid of what he would find out!

So here he was, watchin' as Kane lifted Janie down from Deacon. Makin' over her like she was some breakable china

116

doll. And her, the sheriff, and the best shot in three counties.

Still, lookin' at her, all dainty and feminine in that pretty white, fringed outfit, he couldn't wholly blame the fella. You had to know Janie like he did to know what a tough little bird she could be when she needed to.

The way she was lookin' up at Kane with those liquid blue eyes of hers, so big and trustin' and—Isaac swallowed—so filled with love.

Doggone, there was no other way to express it. It just made him more determined than ever to see that her dear little heart wasn't broken again.

Right then and there he made up his mind.

First thing Monday morning he was going to send off a letter to that bank in New York and find out what he could about this Kane Braxton fella.

If the man truly turned out to be the knight in shining armor that Janie supposed he was, well, Isaac would just have to live with it.

Betty Jean ran up and grabbed his arm.

It embarrassed him a little, her public show of affection. Course, it was a kinda pleasant embarrassment. He knew there were plenty of fellas in Whisperin' Bluff who would have given their eyeteeth to trade places with him. Betty Jean was considered quite a catch in these parts. And he knew why. She was a pretty thing and real generous with her kisses.

That part he liked all right. What red-blooded fella wouldn't?

But in front of other folks, especially Janie, who was always lookin' on with such annoyin' encouragement, he preferred a little more discreet display. Truth be told, he tended to be more a secret pinch and squeeze kinda fella.

Still, he didn't want to hurt her feelin's by makin' her think that her sweet caresses were not appreciated. He'd just suffer in silence.

Sweet sufferin'!

He smiled, looking down into those big, adorin' brown eyes.

For a fella who had once been treated like an outcast, it wasn't a bad feelin' knowin' he was the envy of almost every bachelor in Whisperin' Bluff.

Not a bad feelin' at all!

He squeezed her hand. "You look mighty pretty, Miss Betty Jean."

She was wearing a red and white striped gown with a tiny waist and balloon sleeves and ruffles circling her dainty neck. Her auburn locks were caught in a stiff blue bow at the nape of her neck.

"And very patriotic," he added.

"Oh, Isaac, you're just saying that." She lowered her eyes shyly.

"No, I really mean it. You look just like a flag."

Her head shot up.

Guess that wasn't quite what she'd expected.

"And pretty. *Real* pretty."

She smiled demurely.

That was better.

Sometimes he wished she didn't always expect him to reinforce his compliments with a second soundin', as if hearin' it once was never enough. Some girls were insatiable that way, and he was learnin' Betty Jean was one of them.

That was one of the good things about Janie. You gave her a compliment—not that he often did—but if he did, she just said thank you and went on about her business. She didn't need all that reassurance.

He glanced over at her as she looked up at Kane with that sappy expression in her eyes. He was holdin' on to her like she was infirm. Let the girl stand on her own!

"Come on." He dragged Betty Jean over to where Kane and Jane were still standing. "You were really somethin' up there, Janie, leadin' that parade. You looked real fine."

Jane dragged her gaze away from the struttin' peacock and looked at Isaac as if he'd just interrupted something important. Even though a word wasn't passin' between them.

They were just starin' at each other.

"I was mighty proud of you, Janie girl. And your pa would have been, too."

"Well, thank you, Isaac. That's nice of you to say."

Now that was the way to handle a compliment. No lookin' down and actin' real silly, like it wasn't true when you both knew it was.

"Betty Jean and Ma have a spread out under the oak," he said. "Soon as you two get Deacon back to the stable and pick up Janie's picnic, come on over and join us. We'll save you a spot."

Jane's expression told him that wasn't how she'd planned on spending the afternoon.

Well, too bad. It was for her own good! Until he found out more about this Kane Braxton fella, he was gonna keep him in his sights as much as humanly possible.

Of course, he'd have to be subtle, not be obvious about it. He sure didn't want Janie mad at him again.

❧

Kane and she were a couple. Jane felt that delicious thrill of knowing everyone could see that as he carried her picnic basket and guided her across the meadow, his hand placed possessively at the small of her back.

"Over here, Janie." Isaac waved from the spot he had saved beneath a large, spreading oak on the knoll at the edge of the green.

If she'd had a choice, she and Kane would have found a secluded spot, rather than right there in the middle of everything where Isaac and his mama and Betty Jean had spread their blanket. But it was so sweet of Isaac to have saved a place for them that she didn't have the heart to decline his invitation. It was just another example of how hard he was trying. She was so grateful for all his efforts to bond with Kane that she wouldn't even consider doing anything to disappoint him.

"You can always be counted on to pick the perfect spot,

Isaac." It offered not only a view of the children frolicking down by the creek, but the pickup baseball game and the contests scattered across the meadow. She gazed up the little hill to the vacant lot next to the graveyard. "Perfect for viewing the fireworks, too!"

"I do my best," Isaac grinned.

Kane had just finished spreading their blanket when Big Jim walked by.

"Hey, Jim," Isaac called. "How'd you do in the horseshoe competition?"

The large man paused, smiling. "Managed to retain my title."

"Congratulations. Say, if you don't have a better offer, how about joinin' us for lunch?"

Jane's breath caught. If ever there was a setup this was it. She glanced over at Jackie Lee.

"By all means, Big Jim," Betty Jean twittered. "We'd love to have you join us."

Jackie Lee sat stiff and silent, pretty as a picture in her blue and white dotted swiss gown with the puffed sleeves and ruffled neckline, a warm blush rising in her cheeks.

"If Miss Jackie Lee agrees," Big Jim said quietly.

Jane held her breath.

After a measured moment Jackie Lee lifted her gaze. "Jackie Lee agrees," she murmured softly, moving to make room for him.

Jane gave a great sigh of relief. At last, at last, the moment of silence between them had been broken.

She glanced over at Isaac, but his eyes were on his mama with such tenderness shining in them, and such brightness, that she knew he was blinking back tears, as was she.

Tough guy!

A sudden commotion at the edge of the meadow caught their attention.

"It's Ludd and his cronies, celebrating as usual," Isaac said.

Actually, they were Ludd's ranch hands. Nobody would be

Ludd Morgan's crony unless he was paid to be.

They were racing around the meadow all liquored up, shooting off their mouths and their guns, bullets and "whoopees" flying every which way.

It was a sight!

"Let me take care of it," Isaac said, starting to stand up, but Jane pushed him back down.

"It's my job." She reached for the holster that she'd laid beside the picnic basket. "I can handle it."

Strapping it on, she marched out into the open field, smack in front of Ludd's prancing mare.

"We don't need your kind of celebrating here, Ludd," she shouted over his din.

"Ah, come on, Sheriff, be a sport, it's the Fourth a July."

"I'm being a sport, Ludd, by not throwing you in jail for disturbing the peace. Now you move out on your own, or I'll help you."

"Are you challengin' me, girl?" The man gave a drunken sneer.

"No, I'm promising."

"Oh, yeah?" He whirled his horse in a circle. Then, his rheumy eyes staring belligerently into hers, he lifted his pistol, aiming a round toward the sun.

That did it!

Before he could blink, Jane had drawn her gun and in one motion, shot the pistol clean out of his grimy hand.

Ludd howled and grabbed his wrist.

"Stop your whining, Ludd Morgan. You're not hurt." She marched over to where his weapon had fallen and picked it up. "Now vamoose before I have Spike lock you up."

"I want my gun back."

"You'll get it back when you're sober enough to know when and where to shoot it. Now get, before I lose my patience."

"Not until you gimme my gun back."

Jane stood in the middle of the field, her feet apart, a pistol in either hand. "I'm warning you, Ludd!"

By this time his ragged band of followers was long gone, leaving their leader to fend for himself.

If he hadn't been so dangerous, Jane might have felt sorry for him, his gnarled little wind-whipped body cleaving to the saddle. Sitting there astride his horse in the middle of the meadow, humiliated and alone in front of the whole town.

Ludd rammed his spurs into his roan's flanks and the horse lunged, so close Jane stumbled back. "I'm not gonna forget this, missy. Yer gonna rue the day! You're all gonna rue the day," he shouted, pumping his fist. "You're not gonna forget Ludd Morgan."

With that, the drunken lout whipped the mare on either side of the neck, and she shot forward. A stream of epithets unfurled like a flag behind him.

It had all happened faster than it could be told, and by the time Spike had lumbered down into the meadow to do his part, Ludd had already disappeared.

Jane trudged back across the meadow to cheers. She laughed and doffed her hat to the crowd. Confident and cool, she had once again met her professional challenge and skillfully averted what might have had a dangerous outcome.

It was only then she became aware how fast her heart was beating.

"Good job, Janie," Isaac exclaimed, though he and Kane both stood at the ready, their hands next to their pistols—not to mention Big Jim.

"Yes indeed," the older man agreed, with Jackie Lee and Betty Jean murmuring their assent.

Kane reached out and grabbed her hand. The relief in his eyes spoke louder than words.

"You boys didn't trust me to handle it?"

"Oh, yeah, we did, Janie," Isaac assured her.

"Look at you." Her gaze swept the three men who had yet to uncoil.

Isaac grinned and flopped back down on the blanket. "Just in case, Mighty Mite. Ya gotta let men be men."

Jane shrugged and tossed her curls.

"Good job, Janie," Luke Thompson shouted as he trotted toward the makeshift baseball diamond. "Hey, Isaac, we need you on our team."

"Only if my pal Kane agrees to play," Isaac called back, jumping to his feet.

"Come on, Isaac, he's hardly dressed for it," Jane said in an effort to spare Kane Isaac's good-natured bullying.

"Ah, he's tough, aren't you, Kane?" Isaac challenged.

"Sure, Isaac." Kane grinned at Jane. He leaned down and brushed his pleated trousers. Doffing his finely tailored jacket, he folded it neatly and placed it beside the picnic basket, then systematically rolled up one sleeve, then the other of his pristine white shirt.

Men! Always up for a challenge.

It was so patently obvious, just looking at him, that baseball was not Kane's forte. She knew Isaac had the best intentions, and she was grateful that he was so generous in insisting that Kane be included, but to embarrass him this way. . . How could Isaac be so obtuse? She watched them saunter side by side across the meadow, one tall and blond, striding with such athletic grace; the other, marching beside him, broad-shouldered and muscular, his tousled hair flaming in the noonday sun.

When Kane hit the winning home run over the trees, Jane leaped to her feet, shouting with excitement. She turned to share her joy only to find Betty Jean, alone, jumping up and down beside her.

Jackie Lee and Big Jim had disappeared.

As Kane and Isaac trotted back up the slope, Betty Jean ran forward and threw her arms around Isaac's neck. "You were wonderful. Just wonderful, Isaac."

Jane couldn't help smiling at the way Isaac blushed.

"Kane was the real hero," he said, struggling to disengage the girl's clinging arms. "He hit the home run that brought all us other fellas in to score."

Kane patted him on the back. "It was a team effort, my friend," he said modestly. "I couldn't have done it if you hadn't been on those bases. We needed every run to win."

What a magnanimous gentleman he was. Jane's heart swelled with pride.

Kane looked at her and winked.

The truth was, in all the time she'd known him, he had never seemed more at ease or happier.

Or more handsome, in his soiled white shirt.

"Where's Ma?" Isaac asked.

Jane shrugged.

"Don't tell me she and Jim missed our grand performance."

"Looks that way."

They traded knowing smiles.

Kane's performance throughout the day continued to be just as spectacular, exceeded only by Jane's overwhelming pride. It appeared Isaac had created a monster, for there was hardly a race or contest in which Kane did not enter or excel—even the pie eating contest.

What tickled Jane as much as anything was the expression on Bertha Warner's face when her Harmonizers were defeated in the barbershop quartet competition, and the Monotones took home the prize!

Yes, indeed, by the end of the day, if there was anyone in the community of Whispering Bluff, Colorado, who did not know the name Kane Braxton, he'd been napping.

Wrapped in the warm, velvety darkness, Kane draped his arm around Jane's shoulders, pulling her close as they listened to the snap and pop of the exploding fireworks lighting the sky above the little church, with a sparkling profusion of color.

Jane nestled in his arms, her heart filled to overflowing with gratitude and joy and a deep sense of serenity.

If only this feeling of certainty and peace could last.

Please, God!

twenty

Jane sat bolt upright in bed.

Bells clanging! Shouting voices!

Outside her window.

An eerie yellow glow flickered beneath the blind.

Throwing off the covers, she leaped from her bed, ran over, and threw up the sash.

Light flooded the room. Not the light of morning, but a wild, pulsing light.

Fire!

Through the open window the acrid smell of smoke enveloped her tiny bedroom.

Across the street, Good Shepherd Community Church was an inferno of blazing glory, horrific and beautiful, lighting the night sky with licking flames of orange and yellow and crimson.

Already the fire wagon was racing around the corner.

She leaned out her window. Townsfolk were beginning to converge: men in nightshirts, suspenders holding up their hastily grabbed trousers; women in dressing gowns, their wild locks and plaited hair flying; all frantic in their rush.

She whirled around, glancing at the clock on her dresser as she slid her feet into her slippers.

It was just past midnight.

Shrugging on her robe, she ran down the steps of her cottage and into the street.

Sparks flew everywhere, landing on the bushes and in the grass. The meadow was alight with little bonfires that flared then extinguished in puffs of flying cinders.

Already a fire brigade had begun to form, men and women passing buckets of splashing water hand over hand. Without a word Jane slipped in between Mavis and Pru Pike.

At the head of the line, Kane, his white shirttails flying, heaved water onto the flames, then passed the empty buckets to Pastor Pike who handed them back down the line to be filled again. The mayor, his fire helmet askew, his red braces sagging over his rotund belly, ran up and down the line shouting orders and encouragement over his megaphone; and the children, clustered in little clumps of fear and awe, hugged each other, their mouths agape, as they stared up the blazing building.

Jane recognized Isaac's tousled hair, bright as the flames, as he raced forward with the water hose, his broad chest bare, his muscles bulging, grasping the nozzle in his strong grip. Zeke Pool and Mr. Norwood behind him, helping to maneuver the hose while Cliff Walker manned the pump at the water barrel on the wagon.

Despite the struggle, it soon became evident that the church was lost. The best they could do now was to keep the fire from spreading to the parson's house next door.

Dawn was peeking across the eastern sky before the fire was finally extinguished, the length of hose wound up, the last bucket piled into the wagon, and the weary had straggled back to their beds.

Drooping with fatigue and covered with soot, Jane, Isaac, and Kane collapsed on her front stoop. As the indigo sky turned from pink to azure they gazed in woeful silence across at the charred, skeletal remains of the little church.

"Kane hit another home run," Isaac murmured. "Seems he was the one to report the fire."

Jane turned. "You were?"

He nodded. "I couldn't sleep, thinkin' about the fine day we had." He gazed down at her for a moment. "I was readin' one of Shakespeare's sonnets, actually."

Feeling suddenly self-conscious, she pulled her silky, smudged dressing gown farther across her knees.

He smiled. "My room's on the back, you know, and I just

happened to look up, and saw this flickerin' light. I knew at once what it was."

She linked her arm through his. "I hate to think of what might have happened to the parsonage if you hadn't seen it. It's bad enough the church should burn. But oh, my, what if something had happened to the family." She sighed, resting her head against his shoulder. "I can't even think about it."

Kane reached up and patted her hand.

"Yeah, you're quite a hero," Isaac murmured.

Jane straightened. "Something worries me, though."

Isaac looked over at her. "Other than the fact that we have to find a way to rebuild the church—and come to think of it, start from scratch to find a place for the kids to have their schooling?"

"It's more than that."

"That's not enough?"

"With the school burning down, and now the church. . ."

"It's a coincidence, all right," Kane said. "But at least with this fire you can figure it started from sparks from the fireworks."

"That's what I think and you think, but with Ludd's antics yesterday. . . Folks are already beginning to talk."

Kane frowned. "Do they think he started it?"

"You heard him, yourself. Soundin' off yesterday," Isaac said.

"Yes, but that was just talk," Kane replied. "He strikes me as a little bully with more bark than bite."

"I think you're right," Jane said. "But not everybody sees him that way. And when something like this happens I feel the makings of a mob brewing."

Isaac leaned forward, resting his hands on his knees. "Yeah, you're right. Ludd's mouthin' off like he did is just too convenient."

"You don't think he did it, do you?" Kane asked.

Isaac shrugged. "I don't shoot until I'm sure."

"But Zeke Pool does," Jane said. "And you know what a hothead he can be. He'd get up a lynch mob if he saw half a reason." She looked at Isaac and then at Kane. "It would give me real comfort if I could count on the two of you to be ready, just in case I need a couple of extra deputies."

Isaac looked over his shoulder at her. "You don't even have to ask. You know I'm ready, Janie girl. Same as Kane."

Jane patted his arm. "I figured." She sagged back down into herself again, too tired to move. Although it was silly to keep sitting here when she could be curled up in bed. Yet even as weary as she was, she doubted she could fall back to sleep, her body ached so.

Resting her hand on Kane's shoulder she pushed her stiff self up from the steps. "Well, at least there were two positive things to come out of the day."

"Only two?" Kane whispered, giving her a fond look as he helped her up.

Jane returned a wan smile. It would have been more if she'd had the strength.

Isaac's head shot up. He'd caught the private exchange. "Only two?"

"I saw your mama and Big Jim walking down by the creek."

"Is that so."

"Hand in hand."

Isaac smiled, letting it sink in. "So, what's the other?"

"Bertha Warner got her comeuppance."

Kane frowned. "How's that?"

Isaac grinned. "The Harmonizers lost the barbershop competition."

❧

Jane had had reason to worry. Trouble was brewing. Obviously, she'd been right; not everyone saw the two fires as the sad coincidence that she did.

And Ludd, as she'd anticipated, was the target.

She'd had to use her muscle as sheriff, backed up by Spike and her two newly appointed deputies, Kane and Isaac, to quell the uprising instigated by Zeke.

There were times she got as impatient with that hothead

as she did with Ludd. In his own way Zeke could be just as much of a bully, and probably wielded more influence because he was a more active member of the community. A rabble-rousing one!

She understood the helpless discouragement shared by the community, but on the part of Zeke and his volatile ilk, it too often escalated into rage.

That's why she was so relieved when the mayor and Pastor Pike immediately organized a community meeting before things got out of hand and somebody ended up in the hoosegow. Or worse!

⁊⁊

Kane blocked out the dissonant clamor of agitated voices as he surveyed the city council chamber from the shadow of the entrance. Folks were crowded shoulder to shoulder on the benches and against the three walls facing the podium. The mayor and the city council were lined up in chairs behind it.

Sweet Jane was sitting in the second row between the banker and Isaac.

Her best friend! Ha! Maybe hers, but not his!

That boy had more than friendship on his mind. It showed in his face every time he looked at her. Though thankfully, he didn't realize it.

And Isaac didn't trust Kane, either. That was just as clear. Although the fella tried hard not to show it. Good reason to stick to him closer than the hide on a horny toad. He wasn't about to let the boy get between him and Jane and ruin everything.

Sweet Miss Jane had more than doubled his reason to stay in Whisperin' Bluff. She'd slipped in and wrapped her dainty little hands around his heart and wouldn't let go. Yes, indeed! If ever he'd been handed an excuse to stop his wanderin' ways and set down roots, it was this sweet lady.

He leaned against the jamb of the door, crossed his ankles, and flicked a speck of lint from the cuff of his fine-tailored cutaway.

He enjoyed havin' fine apparel, even in this little town. He took pride in his appearance. Didn't mind at all if people admired him for it. Although he'd made a point of giving them other reasons to think well of him.

He knew it was because of the way he'd grown up that he cared so much about the appearance of things.

He'd tried to put that all behind him, but no matter what, it kept popping to the surface, like oil bubbles to the top of water.

Like now.

Like every time he heard the whistle of a train: The memory would just shoot back like a bullet to the heart, and he'd see the undersized, dirty little urchin in the broken-down shack next to the tracks.

"Poor white trash." That's what folks had called his family.

White trash!

Even now the words were a scab that wouldn't fall off.

"But you're not gonna be like us, boy. You're gonna show 'em," his pa would vow. "You're smart. Yer gonna make somethin' of yourself."

"Your pa is right," Ma would say. "Yer blessed, yes you are. The good Lord has blessed you with specialness." Her face would get all pious, and she'd look up toward heaven and clutch her Holy Bible to her heart like it held the secrets of the universe. And from her poor, simple standpoint, he supposed it did. What else did she have but, as she put it, "the Lord's sacred word."

She certainly didn't hear any sacred words comin' from the mouth of his drunken pa, who blamed her for all his misfortune.

"He has a plan fer ya, son," Ma would say. "You're truly blessed. You never forget that. God's blessed you!"

Ma was right! He was blessed.

He'd been given the brains and the fortitude his pa lacked, and the handsomeness of his mother, back when she was young and pretty, like in the pictures he'd seen of her, not the haggard, beaten-down hag she'd become because of the old man's meanness.

Pa was right about one thing. He wasn't gonna be like them.

He looked out over the chamber.

These folks admired and trusted him. By the end of tonight they would hold him in even greater regard. He was going to see to that.

His gaze lingered on the golden curls of the dearest, most innocent little soul in the whole world. His sweet Jane. If there was justice on this earth, after tonight, she would belong to him, heart and soul.

Him, Kane Braxton!

His moment had come. His dreams would at last be realized.

twenty-one

Jane looked toward the back of the small crowded chamber.

Where was Kane? He'd said he was coming. She'd saved him a place.

"Is this seat saved, Janie?"

The banker. "It's saved for you, Mr. Norwood." She suppressed a sigh and set a smile, moving closer to Isaac as the middle-aged man slid in beside her.

It took three robust hits of Mayor Figg's gavel to quiet the crowd. The mayor's baldpate glowed above the tufts of hair sprouting over his ears like trimmed buffalo grass. Preening in his own self-importance, he folded his fleshy fingers across his massive belly, waiting for everyone's undivided attention.

Still, Jane had to admit, next to his own self-image, Mayor Figg had the best interests of the community at heart.

The mayor cleared his throat, and in the sonorous tones that always bespoke the importance of his pronouncements, he began. "My friends. . ." He paused and surveyed the crowd. "It goes without saying, our little town has suffered a devastating loss—make that two devastating losses: first the schoolhouse, and now the church. Obviously we're going to have to come up with a plan as soon as possible to meet the dual challenge of rebuilding them. To that end, I ordered an emergency meeting of the city council. Tonight, I've called you all here to apprise you of our recommendations."

He cleared his throat. "After deliberation, we concluded that since plans were already underway for the rebuilding of the schoolhouse, we'd start there. I know we'd been planning on a better building than the last one. But if we just rebuild a simple one-room structure like before, we can get it up in no time. That is, if everyone pitches in. That's the consensus of your city council, to go ahead with a simple schoolhouse."

If it could be said in two sentences, the mayor took ten.

"But what about the church?" came a whiny female voice from the rear.

"If you'll be patient, Henrietta, we'll get to that."

The mayor continued. "I'd like to call on Doc Warner, Chairman of the Board, to give you his report on the damages and costs for replacement of the schoolhouse."

Doc Warner rose. He looked every inch the part of the old country doctor in his black frock coat, with his gray, mutton-chop whiskers, and dark, assessing eyes, which now scanned the crowd. "Those of you who have already surveyed the damage know that the building itself was a total loss." His mustache twitched. "The good news. . .the outhouse is still intact."

A ripple of laughter ran through the room.

"As well as the bell. The potbellied stove sustained some damage, but Rush Berry has volunteered to take care of that." Doc nodded at a redheaded man in the first row. "Thanks, Rush." Turning back to the crowd, he continued. "Basically, the schoolhouse was a simple structure: four walls and a roof. If we don't try and get fancy, and rebuild it just as it was, and we get good help from you folks in the community, we figure we could have it up week after next, just as we'd planned."

"What's it gonna cost?" a robust middle-aged man leaning against the east wall called out.

The mayor moved forward. "That depends on all of you."

"Yer Honor!" It was Les Harris, owner of the lumber mill, a slight, shy man with thinning gray hair and the face of a lost hound. He stood staring down at the brim of the straw hat twisting between his fingers.

"Yes, Les?"

"Yer Honor, my brother and me will give y'all the lumber ya need at our cost."

"Why, Les, that's mighty generous of you and Will. Mighty generous! That's what we're talking about, folks. That kind of participation." The mayor led a round of applause as Les, blushing with embarrassment, dropped back into his seat.

Les's wife, Emma, leaned over and gave him an affectionate pat.

Over Emma's shoulder, Jane noticed that Craig Larson had raised his hand. "I'll be glad to act as foreman on the job."

"I'm a roofer," came a voice from Jane's right. "You can count on me."

Isaac raised his hand. "I'll sign on."

Others lent their voices to the call and the excitement grew with the number of volunteers, until it seemed as if everyone was getting into the spirit.

Jane rose. "I'll donate five dollars."

"Put Henrietta and Hazel Pryce on the list for the same," the postmistress called, much to Jane's surprise. They were usually more in the business of criticizing than contributing.

The mayor's wife, Eunice Figg, rose, wearing one of her signature flowered hats: red velvet cabbage roses, with a bluebird garnish. "As president of the Whispering Bluff Garden Club, I have just conferred with our treasurer, Mary Aubrey, and I think we can safely pledge fifteen dollars from our treasury."

"Ten from the Thompsons." Luke Thompson, just down the row from Jane, smiled at his son, Danny.

"Doc and I can match that," called Bertha Warner, who was not about to be outdone.

Mavis Dodd waved a pink hanky. "Two dollars here."

That was a real sacrifice for Mavis, with two children to support alone.

And Betty Jean Gordon, who was sitting on the other side of Isaac and fanning him with her impressive dark lashes, suddenly jumped to her feet. "I can afford a dollar, Your Honor." And everybody clapped.

"We'll have to have Miss Lilly tally up the total," the mayor said when things had quieted down. "But I think we're well on our way."

"What about school supplies?" a woman called from the back.

"That was the next order of business," the mayor said. "Schoolmaster?"

Even though Jane harbored no envy in her heart, seeing John Aubrey standing up there in front, so tall and handsome and serious, that shock of dark hair falling across his noble brow, she had to admit to a twinge of nostalgia.

"Thank you, Mayor Figg," John addressed the mayor, then turned to the audience. "It's the same list I gave you before, since all our new supplies were lost in the fire." He consulted his list. "We'll need slate boards and chalk, pencils, inkwells, ink, pens and paper, and workbooks. If I order them now they should arrive from Denver by the time the building is up."

Jacob Hostetler rose briefly from behind the mayor. "I'll take care of paying for the supplies."

"What about desks?" called a woman standing against the wall.

"Student desks are expensive," John said. "Until we can afford them we will have to make do with planks stretched across sawhorses and nail barrels for seats."

"What do desks cost?" called Big Jim.

Jane turned, to see that he was sitting next to Jackie Lee in a row near the rear.

John thought a moment. "Twenty-five desks—I'd say about two hundred and fifty dollars."

"Done," Big Jim boomed and smiled down at Jackie Lee.

"So what about the church?" Henrietta called again.

"Clearly, we can only handle one thing at a time," the mayor said. "Rebuilding the church is a huge challenge, and a much greater expense."

"Well, where do you expect us to hold services in the meantime?" Henrietta persisted.

At that, Big Jim stood up. "We've been givin' it some thought. And it seems there's only one spot in town big enough to handle the entire congregation at one time, and the choir, and the Sunday school"—he glanced down at Jackie Lee—"and that's the saloon."

An audible gasp echoed throughout the little chamber, then, a stunned silence.

"How sacrilegious can you get?"

"Even to mention such a thing is blasphemy!"

Big Jim continued as if he hadn't heard the two Pryce sisters. "And Jackie Lee's agreed to let us use it."

"Why not?" Luke Thompson rose. "I'm in favor of it. After all, it's only temporary. As Jim says, where else is there that's big enough?"

"But a saloon!" Comments were flying in all directions.

The mayor pounded his gavel. "One at a time. You'll all get your chance."

"What would we do with the poker tables?"

"Pshaw, that's the least of our worries," Hazel Pryce hollered. "What about that disgusting pool table?"

"Where'm I gonna buy a beer?"

What is Otis Dengle doing at the meeting?

"I guess you'll just have to give it up for the time being, Otis," Fred Apple shouted. "I say, go for it, Jim!"

Jane looked over at Isaac who was shaking with silent laughter.

She began to giggle. Think of it. What irony! Jackie Lee August, who had been ostracized by so many of the *good* folks of Whispering Bluff, had offered to become their benefactress.

"May I say somethin'?"

The room fell silent as folks turned toward the source of the mellifluous Southern baritone.

Jane's heart leaped at the sight of the tall, shadowed figure standing in the doorway at the back of the chamber.

"Kane Braxton. Come on down here. Sure, you can speak." As Kane strode forward, the mayor said, "Maybe some of you folks don't know it, but Kane here was the one who reported the fire." He patted Kane on the shoulder. "Saved the parsonage, for sure. Maybe even the whole town."

"Just lucky I was awake and saw it," Kane said modestly.

"Anyone here would have done the same."

"No doubt," the mayor boomed. "But you were the one that did, and the folks of this town are real grateful."

"Hear, hear!" shouted Hitch Chapell, and there was a round of applause.

Kane put up his hands to quiet the crowd. He looked so distinguished and imposing, standing tall and princely, next to the squat little mayor.

Her Kane!

He looked down at her, his eyes crinkling in acknowledgment.

Jane's heart pounded with pride. She glanced at the folks around her. She wasn't the only one who was impressed—except for Isaac, who sat there next to her with his arms crossed and wearing his usual skeptical expression.

"Check the outfit," Isaac muttered.

"You're just jealous because you can't afford such finery," Jane whispered. "Now, hush!"

Kane looked down at the gray felt hat in his hands. "I have a proposition to make."

"Let's hear it," the mayor said.

"I'm willin' to match any funds you folks raise toward buildin' your church."

A collective intake of breath played across the room.

"And to start I want to contribute a little seed money in the amount of three hundred dollars."

He reached into his upper vest pocket and withdrew three bank notes, which he handed to the mayor.

The flustered mayor examined the bills, struggling to believe what he was seeing.

"Hope they're not counterfeit," Isaac muttered under his breath.

"How can you say that?" Jane hissed.

"Just kidding," he whispered back.

She glared at him in silence.

Kane continued. "You good folks of Whisperin' Bluff may be wonderin' why I decided to give this gift to your community."

He bowed slightly toward the mayor. "If I may be allowed to explain."

"By all means, by all means, Kane." The mayor fell back weakly into his chair.

Kane looked down, pondering, weighing his words as he stroked the smooth brim of his hat.

"For the last half hour I've been standing in the back of the chamber listenin' to you all. And I've been impressed. Mighty impressed!"

His soft drawl gave a warmth and sincerity to his tone, and an intimacy. As if he were talking to a group of friends. As, indeed they had become.

"I've traveled all over the world, lived by my wits and my intuition. They've served me well, in fact"—he paused, looking somewhat abashed—"paid off handsomely. But a year and a half ago, I realized that my life was missin' something. I had everything money could buy, but I had no roots, no home, no family." He paused and glanced at Jane.

It was the story he'd shared with her—except the saddest part, losing his young wife.

"On that day my life turned around. I began my quest, and tonight I feel my quest has ended. As I listened to you all and saw your generosity, not only of spirit but of what substance you were able; as I heard your concern for your community, and especially for your children, I was moved. Deeply moved." He shook his head. "And suddenly, standing back there, it occurred to me that perhaps it's providence I landed in Whisperin' Bluff at this very moment, when I can make a difference. Perhaps here, in Whisperin' Bluff, I have found the place where my restless heart can find peace."

Jane was almost sure she saw a trace of tears glistening in his eyes. Or were they a reflection of her own?

A profound silence filled the room and then, from the rear, a single pair of hands began clapping; more joined in, until the room fairly shook with thunderous applause. The crowd rose to its feet.

All except Isaac, who finally did, reluctantly. But only after Jane had stomped on his foot.

Well, the meeting had certainly taken an unexpected turn, with a more than satisfactory ending. Whispering Bluff would have its schoolhouse in short order, and soon, their church would be rebuilt, thanks to a stranger who had become a friend in its time of need.

Kane Braxton was a true blessing!

Mayor Figg banged his gavel to signal adjournment. Folks paused to shake Kane's hand before hurrying out. Most had a piece to go, and it had already gotten dark.

"Will you look at that," Jane breathed as she and Isaac stepped into the brisk night air. "Isn't that the most beautiful horse you ever laid eyes on?"

Kane's stallion was tethered in front, its silky coat gleaming in the moonlight.

Isaac shook his head, and in a voice mimicking a Southern drawl, he said. "Ah just wonder who it belongs to."

"You are so sarcastic, Isaac August," Jane said. "What is wrong with you? Here is a man who has opened his heart—"

"And his wallet," Isaac murmured.

"—to our community and you still haven't got a nice word to say about him."

"I'm sorry, Janie, but I still think there's something that doesn't ring true. He's too smooth."

"He poured out his heart."

"Said what they wanted to hear."

"I can't believe you." Jane shook her head in frustration. "Why, it was the most humble—"

"Too humble."

"How can a person be too smooth and at the same time be too humble?"

"Making that big show of generosity."

"Well, he was generous."

Isaac let out a protracted sigh. "I may be all wrong. I hope I am. I still have an odd feeling."

"You and your odd feelings. From now on keep them to yourself."

"Time will tell." He gave a dismissive wave and ambled up the street toward the saloon. "See you tomorrow."

"Not if I see you first," she grumbled and turned—

Smack into the chest of Kane. Had he not reached out and caught her, she surely would have landed on her fanny.

But instead, she landed in his arms, praying he hadn't overheard her conversation.

twenty-two

The week following the community meeting, Big Jim stayed in town. He and Isaac removed the SALOON sign over the entrance and replaced it with one reading: WHISPERING BLUFF WORSHIP CENTER.

Isaac was boxing bottles of liquor from above the bar, the plan being to fill the shelves with what Bibles and hymnals folks had donated and those that Big Jim had managed to secure.

Jackie Lee was working beside Isaac, sponging the empty shelves with warm, soapy water after he emptied them.

That morning Isaac had received a letter back from the Bank of New York, confirming that Kane did have an account but that their confidentiality policy made it impossible to give him further information.

"So, what did I learn, other than that the fella isn't a pauper? I'm still not satisfied," he confided to his mother.

Jackie Lee put down her sponge. "What would satisfy you, son?"

"I don't know." He shook his head miserably.

"Maybe it's time you decided."

"But for Janie's sake—"

"Precisely. For Jane's sake." She sighed, picked up her sponge, and went back to work.

"He acts like he's runnin' for mayor," Isaac complained. "He shakes more hands than *Hiz* Honor, racin' all over town, callin' meetings, plannin' fund raisers."

Big Jim and Pastor Pike strolled back into the room, wiping their hands on large red bandannas.

"Well, the poker tables are all stowed away," Big Jim said. "Now what do you want us to do about the pool table? There

141

ain't no movin' it so easy!"

"Yoo-hoo!" Eunice Figg's hoarse voice resounded through the room. She, Mary Aubrey, and Bertha Warner were clustered outside, peering over the swinging door, their arms filled with flowers they'd picked for the next day's service.

Jane brushed past them carrying a pair of pewter candlesticks. "For the altar," she called. "They belonged to my mama."

"I've never been in a saloon before," Mary murmured.

"It ain't a saloon anymore, girl," Big Jim boomed. "Didn't you read the sign? Come on in."

Which the women did, with obvious reluctance!

Holding up a damask cloth, Mary asked, "Where shall I put this?"

Bertha looked around. "Where do you propose to have the Sunday school?"

"In Jackie Lee's little eatin' place," Big Jim replied with the pride of a man who had thought of everything. "Of course eventually, when the church is rebuilt, it'll *all* be an eatin' place."

Bertha's eyes narrowed. "You seem to have taken a powerful interest. Does that mean you and Jackie Lee August are going to be business partners?" Her pursed lips reflected disapproval.

"Ya could say that, I suppose." Big Jim winked at Isaac.

Eunice sniffed. "I don't see an altar."

Jackie Lee came forward, the color in her cheeks heightened. "I thought we might cover the pool table and use it for the altar."

Mary turned to Eunice. "That's what my cloth is for."

"Well, that beats all," Bertha harrumphed. "A pool table for an altar."

Pastor Pike gave her a benign smile. "'Now therefore perform the doing of it; that as there was a readiness to will, so there may be a performance also out of that which ye have.' Second Corinthians 8:11, if you care to verify it, Bertha."

Bertha's lips tightened. "You're the expert, Pastor, I'm sure."

Mary cleared her throat. "I hope my cloth is large enough."

"Let's check." Jackie Lee took one end from Mary and together they spread out the elegant white damask cloth over the board-topped structure. "It's perfect! Who'd ever know it was a pool table?"

Jane placed the candlesticks on either end. "But we have no cross."

"In my spare time. . ." Isaac reached under the bar, retrieved a piece of coarse muslin, and unwrapped a simple pine cross. "I whittled this." He strode over and placed it between the two candlesticks, then stood back and cocked his head, studying it with prideful scrutiny. "Not bad, if I do say so myself."

"Oh, Isaac, it's lovely," Jane breathed, running her fingers reverently over the smooth surface of the traditional Latin cross he'd carved with such meticulous and loving care.

She put her arm around his waist, and he likewise, around hers, their heads tilting close.

"What made you think of such a thing?" she asked.

"I don't know. I just did."

"Well, it was brilliant." She kissed his cheek. "So beautiful."

A pulsing awareness spread through him as he gazed into her smiling blue eyes and felt the warmth of her little body in the crook of his arm. The feeling was both familiar and surprising. Familiar, because it was so natural; surprising, because he had never been so keenly aware of her softness before.

Carelessly she withdrew and whirled toward the door. "Got to go. I promised Spike I'd pick up the mail. See you all in church tomorrow."

Big Jim rubbed his palms together. "How do you want the chairs set up, Pastor, with a center aisle? Don't look like there'll be enough, though. Reckon we'll have to make some benches."

The ladies got busy, too, arranging the flowers in containers they'd brought.

But Isaac wasn't paying attention to the activity going on around him. He was looking past the swinging doors and contemplating what he had so suddenly just experienced.

❧

Four days later, Wednesday, to be exact, early evening, Jane was in her office sorting through some papers when Isaac burst through the door.

"We need you up at the saloon, Janie."

"It's not a saloon anymore, Isaac. Remember?"

"You're right!" He grinned. "We need you up at the worship center."

"Is it sheriff business?"

"Let's just say it's business for the sheriff."

"Very well."

Why is he being so evasive?

Quickly, she shoved the papers into the file drawer of her desk. "I'll have to tell Spike I'm going, so he can keep an eye on Otis."

"Otis is back?"

Jane shrugged. "Since your mama's is no longer serving, Otis is now creating his own libation. This afternoon he was making a nuisance of himself at the barbershop, so I had to lock him up. He's still sleeping it off." She reached for her jacket. "Spike!"

There was a grumble from the back room.

"I'm leaving for a spell. Will you keep an eye on Otis?"

The rumpled deputy stumbled out, rubbing his eyes.

"Were you taking a nap? I'm sorry."

"S'all right, Sheriff. Sure. I'll watch out for him."

"Come along, Janie." Isaac grabbed her hand, pulling her out into the street.

"What's your hurry?"

"You'll see."

He pushed open the swinging doors of the worship center and ushered her inside.

The room was dim, lit only by candles. Pastor Pike stood before the altar, with Big Jim and Jackie Lee standing in front of him.

Big Jim wore a fine suede jacket and Jackie Lee was—well,

Jackie Lee was like a lovely, full-blown pink rose, from her ruffled skirt, to her still slender waist, to her lace-trimmed sleeves, to the pink bow atop her soft, upswept corn-silk curls. There was a joy about her that pervaded the whole room.

Jane's breath caught.

Jackie Lee hurried toward her and grasped her hand, pulling her forward. "I hope you don't mind this surprise, Janie dear."

"I wanted a big showy weddin'," Big Jim boomed. "I wanted the whole world to know that Jackie Lee was finally mine." He strode up behind her, throwing his big arms around her and squeezing the little woman in a bear hug. "But she said no! Absolutely not! She only wanted those here that she cares about most and who care most about her. And that's you, Miss Janie, and her boy." He grinned, nuzzling the top of Jackie Lee's curls. "You can already see who's runnin' the show."

Jackie Lee reached up and stroked his cheek. "I told you, dear; when we get back from our honeymoon you can have any kind of celebration you want."

Jane could hardly get the words out she was so choked with emotion. "Well," she finally managed, "well, it's about time."

"That's what I say," Big Jim boomed.

Pastor Pike, who had been standing quietly through all this, cleared his throat. "Well, then, I suggest we don't wait a minute longer."

They gathered in front of the altar: Isaac standing beside Big Jim, Jane beside Jackie Lee, Jackie Lee's trembling hand captured in Big Jim's large paw as if he feared his little bird might fly away.

"Dearly beloved. . ."

Jane watched through a blur of tears as Big Jim and Jackie Lee gazed into each other's eyes with a naked devotion, bare of guile or subterfuge. Their voices were husky with emotion as they repeated the vows they had waited almost a lifetime to speak.

"I now pronounce you man and wife."

Big Jim did not wait to be told to kiss the bride, and he

certainly wasted no time in lingering good-byes. Just bear hugs all around, and then he swept Jackie Lee out of there and into his waiting buggy faster than a blink.

Jane, Isaac, and Pastor Pike stood on the steps watching the buggy disappear around the corner.

"Where are they going on their honeymoon?" Jane asked.

Isaac dropped his arm around her shoulders. "To visit her wedding present."

Jane frowned and cocked her head. "And what might that be?"

"A gold mine Jim's uncle left him in Eldora."

"Well that's original." Pastor Pike laughed.

"That's what Jim thought," Isaac said.

Jane giggled. "Does Jackie Lee know what it is?"

"All she knows is they're taking a sleeper railcar west."

"I must say, this has been an amazing day." Pastor Pike shook his head. "And a joyous one!"

As far as Jane was concerned it was still sinking in; the wedding had all happened so quickly.

Come to think of it, not so quickly, really. They'd been waiting a lifetime. At least Big Jim had.

"Will you be locking up?" the pastor asked Isaac.

He nodded.

"Well, I'll be off, then. Pru's waiting supper."

"Have a good evening," Jane offered, knowing her own couldn't get much better.

They watched him go, Isaac's arm still draped around Jane's shoulders. He seemed to have turned awfully quiet.

"What are you thinking?" she asked.

He brushed his cheek against her hair. "I'm thinkin' it's a good thing when someone finds their true love—and recognizes it. Poor Ma had to wait a long time before she did."

"But she did, finally, and that's what counts."

"I can't help thinkin' of all those wasted years with Pa. And Jim was right there, waitin' for her all the time."

Jane turned and looked him full in the face. His blazing hair and endearing features were softened by the dusk.

"They were sad years, that's true, Isaac. But I've said it before, and I'll say it again, as many times as I need to." She allowed both arms to circle his waist. "Your mama does not think of them as wasted. They brought her you."

Suddenly Isaac pulled her close, holding her tight against him. And he was kissing her. Kissing her with a fervor that sent her spinning. Hot, moist kisses—yearning, passionate kisses.

At first she was too surprised to react. Coming to her senses, she jerked back.

"Isaac!" She pushed him away.

Eyes wide, his hands flew out, palms open as if he'd been burned. "I'm sorry! I'm so sorry, Janie. I didn't mean to do that."

It was another one of those times when she knew she should be angry with him, but he looked as shocked as she.

"It was just that, it was just that. . .well, doggone," he babbled, "I don't know what came over me."

"I certainly hope I didn't do anything that might lead you to believe—"

"Never! Never, Janie! Why. . .you and me are just like a pair of old shoes—"

"Well thank you very much for that." She feigned insult, trying hard herself to deflate the embarrassing situation.

"You know what I mean."

She sighed and shook her head. "Of course I do. That's why I can't understand what possessed you." Though deep inside she suspected she had an inkling—of something she had to nip in the bud.

Still, she couldn't bear to hurt him. And the thought of losing his friendship, well that was unbearable, too.

There was something in his expression that made her know she needed to reassure him.

"You and I have something so special, Isaac. I value it with all my heart. I treasure you with all my heart. I just don't want anything to ruin it by—I couldn't bear it if. . ." She was surprised to realize that her voice was quivering and her eyes were moist. "I couldn't bear to lose you."

"Hey, Janie, don't cry." He wiped away a tear that had dribbled down her cheek.

"I'm not crying," she sniffed.

He wrapped his arms around her. In a brotherly way. "I'm not goin' anywhere, Mighty Mite." He leaned back and looked down at her. "It was just a little kiss. You're takin' it all too serious. Let's just forget it."

She nodded.

"We'll just move on, like it never happened. Okay?"

"Okay."

He released her and took her hand. "I've got to get you back, or Spike'll be on my tail—It never happened, right?"

"Right."

He drew her down the steps. Hand in hand they strolled back down Main Street toward her office.

After a moment Jane began to laugh.

"What's so funny?"

"Just for the record, you're a pretty good kisser."

Isaac stopped. "Well, thank you, Janie."

"Not that I'm much of an expert."

"Not until lately," he muttered under his breath.

"That wasn't necessary."

"Sorry, I couldn't help myself."

"Anyway. . ." She resumed walking. "It makes me think you've had a whole lot more experience than you've told me about."

"I should hope so!" Isaac grinned.

Usually, when he left her, Isaac leaned over and gave her a peck on the cheek. It was as if he were about to, then he pulled back and squeezed her hand. "Well, night, Janie."

"Good night, Isaac." She watched him turn and walk back up the street, and then break into a run as if something were chasing him.

They didn't see each other much the next couple of weeks, and when they did that moment was never mentioned.

That isn't to say Jane didn't think about it. She did, more often than she wanted to admit. And it made her sad. She realized that Isaac yearned for that one special person as much as she once had. Before Kane came into her life.

That's why that kiss had happened. With all the emotion of his mama getting married, he had a moment of yearning and Jane was just the girl who happened to be there.

That's what Jane told herself.

It could just as well have been Betty Jean. Well. . .maybe not Betty Jean.

twenty-three

Two weeks after Big Jim and Jackie Lee's wedding, Isaac came rushing into Jane's office. "You'll never believe this!"

She swung around in her desk chair and looked up at him. "The gold mine Big Jim gave Jackie Lee just hit a rich vein and should start showing a profit within a few months."

"How did you know that?" Isaac scowled down at her.

"He telephoned you, didn't he?"

"Well, yes."

"What time is it?"

Isaac looked up at the clock mounted on the wall above Jane's desk. "Ten thirty."

"Yes, and the gossip mavens meet at ten."

Isaac nodded. "They're better than the telephone, telegraph, and the mail put together."

Jane grinned. "I just happened to be looking out my window and knew something was up when I saw them all running out of the post office."

Isaac made a face. "Scatterin' like fleas on the back of a stray hound."

"You got it." Jane smiled.

"Shucks. I wanted to surprise you."

"Sorry."

Isaac leaned against her desk. "They're coming home at the end of the week."

She added raised brows to her smile.

"You knew that, too!"

❧

Over the telephone, Big Jim had promised Isaac a surprise, and nobody in town was about to miss it!

It was warm, even by late September standards. In the

swell of the noonday heat, the townsfolk and their children clustered under the overhang and on the steps of the temporary Whispering Bluff Worship Center, fanning themselves and chatting as they awaited the arrival of Big Jim and Jackie Lee.

Jacob Hostetler stood on the lower step, mopping his brow and the back of his neck. Beside him, Peter used his straw hat to fan himself and Becca. He was beaming, wouldn't let his wife out of his sight—or his arms—he was so happy to have her home for good.

Jane ran over and gave her friend a hug. It was the first time she'd seen her since she'd arrived back after graduating from medical school.

The whole Apple clan had driven out from their farm, even old Granny Apple had come along, dressed in her usual black and leaning on her cane.

Cotton Smather was there, Mavis and her two children. Otis Dengle had shown up with his family, his poor wife holding a still-nursing infant. Jane suspected they were there more for the food than anything else. And Trudy St. Cyr and her son. . .

All the businesses in town had closed, which meant that all the merchants were there: the Mortinsons, the Pools, Cliff Walker, and Cutter Molten with their wives. Hardly anybody was missing.

Henrietta had closed the post office for the afternoon, and even Hazel had come, figuring no one would be making any telephone calls anyway.

The Garden Club members had gathered as a group at the top of the steps: Eunice Figg's wide-brimmed flowered hat, shielding not only her from the sun's rays, but Bertha Warner on one side, and Lilly Johnson on the other. Or so it appeared.

Jane could hardly contain her excitement as she stood between Kane and Isaac on the steps with the rest of the choir: Betty Jean, the Aubreys. . .

Suddenly, Danny Thompson began to jump up and down and point. "Here they come. Here they come."

As Big Jim's buggy drew up in front of the worship center, Pru lifted her baton and the choir burst into "Love Divine, All Loves Excelling" in four-part harmony.

After a moment of obvious surprise, Big Jim hopped down from his yellow-wheeled conveyance and ran around to Jackie Lee's side, making a big show of lifting out his beaming, pink-clad bride and carrying her up the steps to cheering and applause. But hardly had he deposited her at the top, when Mayor Figg rushed forward with a proclamation—which was blessedly short. Then, with great fanfare he ushered them through the flower-swagged entry.

Jackie Lee and Big Jim stopped, transfixed.

The large room had been transformed. Flowers were everywhere. Garlands drooped over the windows and the doors. Bouquets of blossoms hid the bar and spilled over the pool table altar. Rose petals carpeted the pine-planked floor.

Eunice Figg, in a show of conciliation and support, had ordered the members of the Garden Club to strip their gardens. Even Bertha Warner had grudgingly complied.

And under the window the ladies of the Good Shepherd Community Church had laid out a sumptuous repast.

"Oh, my. Oh, my," Jackie Lee breathed, clasping her hands to her bosom. "This is all for us?"

For his part, Big Jim, always a man of measured words anyway, was speechless.

By now, everyone had crowded into the large room, packed together around Big Jim and Jackie Lee or bunched in groups at the serving table.

Pastor Pike stepped forward and raised his hands for attention.

It took a moment for the room to quiet as the mamas corralled their toddlers, and in some cases their teens; and Henrietta, glaring at the Apple twins, gave a loud "Shush" that echoed throughout the room and got everyone's attention, not just the twins'.

Pastor Pike smiled at Jackie Lee and Big Jim. "This is a joyous day for us all as we celebrate the nuptials of our dear friends, and welcome them home."

"Hear, hear," shouted Jacob, Big Jim's best friend.

The pastor clasped his hands, waiting for the applause to end. "Now, as we prepare to partake of this beautiful banquet that our ladies have provided, let us bow our heads."

There was the usual rustle of shuffling feet and folding hands, the whispered admonitions to the children, the expectant silence.

"Our heavenly Father, source of all that is good and beautiful, we come to You with hearts filled with joy and gratitude to celebrate the marriage of our dear friends, Jim and Jackie Lee. May Your infinite love be reborn in each of us as we see it reborn in them.

"Help us to forget our petty aspirations and prejudices, our selfish aims and impatient tempers, and to treat each other with a charitable heart and the love and acceptance that You have taught us. May we serve You with a renewed spirit as we partake in the bounty that You have so generously provided. We ask all this in Your holy name. Amen."

Murmured amens were followed by an immediate clamor as folks pushed forward to crowd around the food-laden table.

That Pastor Pike is a sly one! "Forget our prejudices. . .treat each other with a charitable heart." Jane hoped that the good folks of Whispering Bluff had gotten his message, especially the hens that loved to peck away at the post office.

Her eyes misted as she looked over and saw the joyous Jackie Lee graciously acknowledging the greetings and returning the warm hugs from folks who once had paid her little heed.

Perhaps she really had won them over by her example of the Lord's love.

Since Jane helped attend the food, she and Kane were among the last to be served before finding a spot at a table in the far corner of the room. Their empty plates now lay in front of them.

Jane broke off a bite from her piece of Mavis' dark chocolate cake and popped it into Kane's mouth, saving the last morsel for herself.

He leaned over and brushed a crumb from her lower lip. "I'd kiss it off if there wasn't such a crowd," he whispered.

"Oh, Kane." She shook her head demurely. "You're hopeless."

"You're right. I'm hopeless about you, my sweet Miss Janie."

How could she resist the tingling touch of his hand, the tenderness of his lazy gaze?

"Kane! Kane Braxton!" Big Jim's voice boomed from across the room. "Ah, there you are. Come on over here, boy! I have somethin' for you." Folks were gathering around him.

Now that he'd finally captured his true love, Big Jim seemed a man transformed. Where once he'd been measured, even reticent in his speech, he was now loquacious and outgoing. As if his passions found, could not be contained.

"By now I figure you've all heard the good news about my darlin's weddin' gift strikin' it rich." He gazed down fondly at Jackie Lee, standing close beside him. "Seems only fair, since I struck it rich when I got her."

Everyone smiled.

"My darlin' wanted to share her good fortune with all of you. So, Kane, this is from Jackie Lee and me." He handed Kane a flat, oblong metal box. "With all your work, plannin', meetin's, and raisin' money, she and me thought you should be the one to do the honors."

Kane gazed down at the box, hesitated, then held it out toward Jane. "You open it, Miss Jane," he murmured.

A wide grin split Big Jim's craggy features as he watched Jane undo the latch and lift the lid.

Jane gulped. "Oh, my!"

The crowd leaned forward. Big Jim could always be counted on for a surprise.

This time he'd outdone himself.

"There's thirty of 'em in there, Kane. Thirty hundred-dollar bills. With what the folks have raised and your matchin' funds, and now that the schoolhouse is up and runnin', we can start rebuildin' our little church right away. Better than ever."

Kane stared at the contents of the box.

Jane had never seen the tall, suave, love of her life at a loss for words. Or his face such a montage of emotions.

He looked at Big Jim. "This is—this is amazin'!"

"Ain't it!" Big Jim boomed.

"I—I never anticipated it could happen so fast. That the money could be collected so quickly."

Mayor Figg stepped forward. "Let's hear it for Big Jim!"

Everyone began to cheer and clap.

Big Jim beamed. "Let's hear it for Kane," he boomed. "No way we could have raised the money without him."

Just like Big Jim to shift the attention away from himself.

More cheers drowned out anything else he might have said.

Kane looked from Jane to Big Jim, disbelief still glazing his expression. He raised a hand for silence. "You are amazin'. Simply amazin'." His voice was soft, almost reverent, his Southern accent all the more pronounced. "I can think of no other word for it. And now, Mr. Norwood, I'd feel much easier if this was safely tucked away in our special deposit box with the rest of the money. And I need to write a draft on my New York bank for the matching funds."

The excited group cheered again as the lanky middle-aged banker stepped forward, his black hair neatly parted in the middle, his precisely trimmed mustache and his gold-rimmed pince-nez tightly nipping his nose.

Jane's heart pounded with pride as she gazed up at Kane, the man she had come not only to love, but to admire.

Behind him, she caught sight of Isaac, standing alone. The bittersweet expression on his dear face was one of poignant acceptance. Nevertheless, as he walked toward them she held her breath.

To her surprise, when he reached Kane, he extended his hand. "I'm afraid I haven't always given you your due, Kane. I apologize for that. I see now, you are the man Janie thinks you are."

Kane looked uneasy. "You embarrass me, my friend." His face reflected his discomfort. "I fear you and Miss Jane greatly exaggerate my virtues."

"That's not so," Jane whispered, seizing his arm.

Mr. Norwood intervened. "Shall we take care of our business?"

Kane nodded. "I'll be right along." He cleared his throat and turned back to Isaac. "I want to thank you for your kind words, Isaac. And your friendship! I know how much you mean to our Janie."

Isaac glanced at her. "I appreciate that," he murmured.

But already Kane had moved to follow Mr. Norwood. "This shouldn't take long, Janie," he called over his shoulder. "I'll be back shortly to help clean up and walk you home."

She and Isaac watched as Kane braided his way through the crowd, acknowledging compliments, shaking hands. Ever the charming, Southern gentleman!

"That was kind of you, Isaac." She turned and looked up at him. The tears that she'd been forestalling suddenly hazed her vision. Gazing into his dear, kind face, she realized what a price he had just paid. He'd done it for her, to set her heart and mind at rest.

What greater friend could she have?

He didn't reply, just gazed down at her with a pensive smile. What more was there to say?

By now the folks were starting to clear out. Big Jim and Jackie Lee had left soon after the presentation, their buggy a bower of flowers from the celebration.

Jane hugged Becca good-bye, promising to see her within the week.

Isaac, Pastor Pike, and John Aubrey stowed away the tables and reset the rows of chairs and benches for the service on Sunday. The church ladies packed up the remains of the buffet and distributed the leftovers between them.

It was late afternoon before they were finished. The room had emptied. All were gone except Isaac.

And Jane!

twenty-four

Where's Kane?" Jane stood by the doorway looking down Main Street. "I'm worried about him. It's been almost an hour and a half since he left. It shouldn't have taken him more than twenty minutes to deposit that money. I hope nothing has happened to him."

Isaac came and stood behind her. "What could have happened?"

"I don't know."

He grinned. "If yer afraid a walkin' home alone, Miss Sheriff, I'd be happy to oblige."

"That's not funny," she said irritably. "This isn't like him." She continued to gaze out into the street. "He was carrying all that money. You don't suppose. . ."

Isaac leaned against the doorjamb and looked down at her. "Certainly you don't think anyone in this town would attack Kane and steal the church money?"

"I can't think of anybody." She frowned. "Except maybe Ludd."

"Yep, there's always Ludd. Always the convenient suspect."

"With reason."

Isaac began to laugh. "Ya don't even know if the money's gone and already you're convictin' poor Ludd."

"You're right. It's ridiculous."

"Maybe Kane sprained his ankle and is nursin' it back at Miss Trudy's boardinghouse," Isaac suggested.

"If it were something like that he would have sent someone to let me know. No, something happened." She grabbed her sunbonnet. Tying it on, she pushed through the swinging door. "I'm going to find out where he is."

"I'll come with you," Isaac said, following her down the

steps. "Where are you goin'?"

"To Trudy's, of course."

"Takin' the shortcut?"

"Naturally."

Lifting her skirt, Jane hurried between the worship center building and the barbershop where she picked up the little path that meandered through the woods, parallel to Main Street. Isaac was beside her, helping her over the ruts, taking her arm as they forded the creek just past the Aubreys' cottage.

Even though he always offered great moral support, this was one time she would have preferred to handle the situation alone. But she knew it would be unseemly for her to check on Kane by herself; unless, of course, it was official business.

She remembered the day she'd seen Kane right there, where her foot was now stepping, the heart-stopping, handsome stranger lounging on the bank beneath the willow. Lounging there smiling up at her. . .how she'd almost fallen. . .and had been falling ever since.

Was that just five months ago?

Isaac sprinted ahead and took the front steps of the large, three-story boardinghouse two at a time. Impatiently he clanged the knocker.

Just as Jane reached his side, the door opened.

Trudy stood in her red and white apron, a rolling pin in her fist, a smudge of flour on her cheek.

"It's zee sheriff, Janie, and Isaac. Come in. Come in." She looked up demurely at Isaac while letting Jane pass. "It seems I just see you a few hours ago."

Trudy was an immigrant who cultivated her French accent along with her pouty lips and fluttering lashes, which she employed now with Isaac.

"Jane is concerned about Kane," Isaac said.

"He was supposed to be back at the worship center over an hour ago, but he didn't show up," Jane explained.

Isaac shoved his hands into the back pockets of his jeans. "We wondered if you'd seen him."

"No." Trudy shook her head. "But sneak up he could, without me knowing. He has his outside steps, you know. Maybe he has zee bad stomach from Bertha Warner's chicken today. She does not make it in zee French way."

"With wine." Isaac grinned.

Trudy nodded.

Isaac had gotten so wrapped up in being charmed by the Frenchwoman that he'd forgotten what they'd come for.

Jane yanked on his sleeve.

"Oh yes," Isaac said, pulling himself together. "Do you suppose I can go up and see if Kane is in his room?"

Trudy shrugged. "It's okay wiz me, Isaac." She tossed her black curls and fluttered her painted lashes. For a woman well into her thirties, she still had a winning way with gentlemen. "His room is at zee end of the hall," she said as Isaac bounded out of the room.

"Don't let me keep you, Trudy," Jane said. "You go back to your baking. I'll just wait here in the parlor. If you don't mind."

"I don't mind at all, Janie. Give yourself comfortable." Trudy pronounced each syllable with French precision.

But instead of going into the parlor, Jane waited impatiently at the foot of the stairs.

"Janie."

She looked up.

Isaac stood at the top of the stairs, his face drawn. "I think you should see this."

A chill of apprehension swept through her. Heart racing, she lifted her skirts and flew up the stairs.

Isaac caught her at the top. "Wait."

But she thrust his restraining hand aside and ran to the room at the end of the hall. The door stood open.

Jane halted in shocked silence. She felt as if all the air had been sucked out of her.

She leaned against the doorframe, weak with disbelief, her mouth slack.

The room was in disarray: bureau drawers agape; the

armoire door hanging open; empty coat hangers scattered about the floor. The room's occupant had been in a mighty hurry to leave.

"This isn't Kane's room," she whispered. "It couldn't be."

"It is, Janie," Isaac said gently, resting his hand on her arm.

She pulled away and stepped across the threshold.

Her head throbbed. Her heart pounded.

She wanted to scream. She wanted to cry. She wanted to feel something.

Kane was gone!

She was numb.

Stumbling across the room, she collapsed in the chair in front of a small pine desk.

Isaac touched her shoulder. "I'm so sorry."

Violently she shrugged away. "Don't tell me you're sorry! You're glad! You wanted it to be this way so you could say 'I told you so.'"

"You don't believe that."

"No, no," she sobbed, dropping her head onto her folded arms on the desk. "Of course I don't believe it."

She felt disoriented, confused. As if she were in some terrible nightmare from which she would soon awaken.

Her distracted gaze caught sight of a crumpled scrap of paper in the wastebasket beside her, its edges burned.

She reached down.

"What is it?" Isaac asked.

"I don't know," she murmured, smoothing it out on the desk. "It looks like part of a map of Colorado."

Isaac leaned over her shoulder. "Yeah. Here's where we are." He pointed to the area around their valley. "Look at this." His finger traced a faint line heading east, away from the railroad. "What do you make of it?"

Her heart just couldn't fathom what her head was telling her.

After a moment, she said quietly, "Do you suppose that's his route?"

"You know it must be, Janie," Isaac said softly.

For a moment longer she stared down at the sheet, still struggling to accept what was becoming patently obvious.

Kane had absconded with the money!

Gone for good!

She jumped up. "We've got to get to the bank."

Blindly, she ran down the stairs, hardly aware of Trudy in the entry as she ran out the front door.

"Hey, wait for me!" Isaac called after her.

The bank was a short block down First to the corner of Main.

By now the sun was low, the shadows long. No one was on the street as she rounded the corner and ran up the steps of the bank, Isaac at her side.

She pushed on the door. It swung open easily. It should have been locked.

From behind the counter they heard a muffled cry.

Mr. Norwood was sprawled on the floor in front of the open vault, trussed tight as a Thanksgiving turkey, a gentleman's white linen handkerchief tied tightly around his mouth. His face was red; his eyes, bulging. Beside his head lay his shattered spectacles.

Around him, the safe deposit boxes were scattered in careless disarray, empty as the drawers in Kane's bedroom.

Isaac pulled the gag from the banker's mouth, releasing a stream of expletives from the distraught man.

Who could blame him?

Kane had betrayed him—as he had betrayed them all.

Isaac helped Mr. Norwood to his feet as Jane turned and ran out the door.

Isaac caught up with her. "Let me handle this, Jane."

"You're not the sheriff." She pushed past him. "I am. It's my job!"

As she entered the office, Spike shoved the book he was reading into the bottom drawer and leaped to his feet.

Grabbing hold of her shoulders, Isaac spun her around. "Be

sensible, Jane. It's just not practical for you—"

"Because I'm a woman?" she spat. "I'm the best shot in—"

"I know, three counties. That's not the point. It's. . .well, it's the circumstances. You and him. . ."

Which was precisely the reason she wanted to face him.

"What if he were to get away? What would folks say then?" His voice gentled. "Look, Janie, let Spike and me get up a posse. John Aubrey, Big Jim, maybe Luke Thompson. We can move fast, Janie. And the onus won't be on you."

Jane stared up at him. "All right," she said after a moment. "I'll stay here. But you'd better get started. It'll be dark soon."

Isaac let out a breath of relief. "After all, we know which direction he's headin'."

twenty-five

As soon as the quickly assembled posse headed east out of town, Jane saddled Deacon and headed toward the setting sun.

Kane was too smart to leave as obvious a clue as a partially burned map, unless it was intended to mislead.

She was almost certain his plan was to go toward the mountains, along the creek that fed Rikum's Pond. She remembered the day they'd picnicked there, when he'd first come to Whispering Bluff, how he'd been so interested in the surrounding terrain and especially the creek and where it came out of the mountains.

She'd thought it just idle interest. But even then, he was planning his escape route.

She spotted fresh hoofprints. Her instinct had been right.

As she guided Deacon along the trail, her thoughts were a battleground of rage, recrimination, and regret. She had loved him so much, the devotion in his silver eyes, the melting murmur of his voice, his kisses. . . Even now, even now, the thought of them sent a tremor of forbidden heat surging through her body.

Oh, the shame of it!

The humiliation!

How could she have been so deluded, so deceived?

Why, he was nothing but a flimflam artist of the most reprehensible kind, the kind that preyed on women and stole their love and trust. To say nothing of the fact that he was a thief.

With darkness falling, she had reached the fork in the trail. She reined in Deacon, dismounted, and pulled a small lantern from her saddlebag, lit it, then leaned down to examine the loamy earth. The hoofprints continued, following the creek path.

She extinguished the light, shoved the lantern into her saddlebag, and sprang back into the saddle.

She looked up at the intermittent clouds that swept the moon, and considered her advantage. He'd gotten a good head start. But with the sagebrush closing in, slapping and tugging, and tree roots waiting to trip his horse, he was almost certain to stop for the night and start up again at dawn.

Suddenly, a nearby whinny split the silence.

"Shh, boy," she whispered, leaning forward and stroking Deacon's neck. "Shh!"

They sat melded together, still as a statue, listening. One minute, two ticked by. Nothing! She dismounted and looped her Deacon's reins over a drooping branch.

Moving forward, she paused, listening again for the crackle of leaves, the break of a twig. But she heard only the gurgle of the creek, the whisper of the breeze, and the soft *coo* of a besotted turtledove in the tree above her.

Finally satisfied, she made her way up a slight rise. She would circle around and approach him from behind.

Several minutes passed before Jane sighted the silhouette of the stallion drinking from the moon-dappled creek. She crouched in the brush on the bank above, scanning the clearing.

A few yards beneath her, she caught a glint of light. Kane's rifle! He lounged against his saddlebags—his fat saddlebags stuffed with the town's money—his rifle lying across his knees.

Certainty and strength surged through her. This was her job. This was what she was called to do!

"Throw down your gun, Kane!"

He whirled around, bringing up his weapon.

"Janie. . . Janie, is that you? Are you alone?"

"Don't Janie me. Just toss away your rifle. Now!"

"You wouldn't shoot me, honey." His voice was caressing as he came to his feet.

Her bullet twanged off the trunk of the tree behind him, just inches above his ear.

"Now unhook your holster and throw it on top of your rifle, and step back. Farther!" The moon had come out from behind the clouds and she could see him clearly.

"Ah, Janie." But he did as she'd ordered, slowly, looking around him, searching the thicket. "How did you know where I'd headed?"

"Did you really think I was stupid enough to follow that bogus clue?"

"I never thought you were stupid," he said quietly. "I guess I was stupid to hope I could fool you."

Jane laughed harshly. "You did that all right."

"Havin' a trustin' heart doesn't make you a fool, Janie. Where's the rest of your posse?"

"Stop calling me Janie."

"I'm sorry. Come out where I can look at you."

Carefully Jane stepped down the crumbling bank, her gun leveled at him. "You're a smooth one, all right. I'm guessing this isn't the first time you've pulled a stunt like this."

She hated that he still had the power to make her breath catch.

"Can't say as I've ever been quite so ambitious before. Nothing to get me on the wanted posters, anyway." He shook his head. "But when the opportunity presented itself, it just seemed like it was meant to be."

"You set those fires!"

He didn't answer.

"Well, did you?"

"Not the schoolhouse. But the way the folks all rallied around, that gave me the idea." He gave her a long look. "I saw it as my big chance. If I played my cards right I could milk that little town dry, start a new life somewhere else. Become what everyone in Whispering Bluff thought I was." His eyes gleamed.

"There was more to be had, Kane; you took off too soon!" she said bitterly.

"A pretty little sheriff got in the way," he murmured softly.

His gaze was beseeching. "The truth is, Janie, I came to care about you. Way too much." He took a step forward.

"Stay where you are."

He sagged back. "I might still be there if Big Jim hadn't handed me that box of money this afternoon. I looked at you, and I looked at it, and I knew I had to leave right then and there, or I'd never be able to. And then you and the rest of them would find out I wasn't the rich Southern gentleman you all thought I was."

Jane couldn't believe what she was hearing. "Those folks didn't admire you because of what they thought you had, Kane. They admired you for the kind of man they thought you were."

He gazed at her intently, his perfectly angled features sculpted by the moonlight.

"It's not too late, Janie," he said quietly. "Come with me. You can help me become that man."

She stared at him in disbelief.

Was this the man she had thought was her own true love, the man to whom she'd given her heart, not to mention her respect? How could this beautiful face and strong, virile body be so empty of soul and conscience?

"Lie facedown. Put your hands above your head."

"Janie, don't."

"Do as I say." There was steel in her voice and in her heart. She felt nothing for him. Not even Christian charity.

She pulled the handcuffs from her belt and walked toward him.

"You're takin' a real gamble if you think you can get those cuffs on me without me takin' you down, Janie."

"I don't think so, sucker," Isaac's voice boomed out of the darkness. "The lady's done right well so far. I think if I were you, I'd do what she says." He strolled into the clearing.

Jane was shocked at the floodgate of relief and emotion that spilled over her at the sight of him.

"Ah, the cavalry has finally arrived." There was a note of

sardonic resignation in Kane's tone.

"I can handle this," Jane muttered to Isaac.

After all, she did have her pride.

"I know you can, sweetheart. You go ahead. I'm just here to back you up. Like always."

Kane had dropped to his knees and was now lying belly down in the dirt.

"Put your arms behind you," Jane commanded. Then she snapped the cuffs around his wrists.

Isaac sauntered up and leaned over him, putting his face close to Kane's. "You should thank me, Kane. My showin' up probably saved your life. This little sheriff might have had to shoot you if you didn't do what she said."

Jane was struggling to maintain her composure. Now that Isaac had arrived she was struck with how foolhardy she had been to think she could handle this alone.

When she could trust her voice, she asked, "How did you know to follow me?"

Isaac shrugged. "Well, I started out in the posse with the boys, and then I got to thinkin', Janie gave up too easy. Knowin' you, you had to have somethin' up yer sleeve. So I told 'em to go on and I circled back. It was Mavis who told me which way you'd headed. Said she you saw you out her back window. Then I remembered when Kane and me were fishin' at the pond, how he looked things over and asked questions. And then when I saw Deacon hitched up there on the trail, I knew I was right." He gave her a poke. "Two great minds."

"Yes!" she murmured, not knowing how to feel at the moment.

Isaac nudged Kane with the toe of his boot. "I'd like to give ya a good kick, *old friend*, but I'm afraid I couldn't stop there!" He yanked the man to his feet. "Let's git this garbage to jail where he belongs."

twenty-six

Jane didn't look at Kane when the U.S. Marshal escorted him out of her office.

He wasn't the only one she didn't want to look at. For the last weeks she hadn't wanted to look at Henrietta, or Eunice, or the rest of the gossip mavens. She hadn't wanted to see Becca and Peter, or the Aubreys, or Pru and Pastor Pike, or Jackie Lee and Big Jim, or even dear Mavis.

She couldn't bear it when folks gazed at her with that sorrowful, sympathetic expression on their faces and stopped talking because, she knew, they had been talking about her. "Poor Jane!" Almost as if she had some incurable disease.

But most of all, she didn't want to see Isaac!

She couldn't bear the thought—even though she knew he cared and wanted her to be happy, and was always there when she needed him—the thought that deep down he was thinking, *I warned her! I told her!*

So, she'd avoided them all. She went to her office, did what was necessary, and went home to spend her evenings alone, desperately sad and sorry for herself.

After a while, though, wallowing in self-pity gets pretty wearisome. Jane could live with hate, humiliation, and heartbreak for only so long.

One evening, while sitting at her kitchen table, tracing circles with her fork around her uneaten supper, it occurred to her that the time had come to pull herself together. If she was going to move on with her life, she'd better get rid of all this hate that had been festering inside her, sapping her energy, stealing most of her waking thoughts. That, at least, she could do.

Time would have to handle the heartbreak and humiliation.

She pushed her plate aside and stood up.

168

As she shoved open her back screen door and stared out into her moonlit garden, she remembered a sermon Pastor Pike had given one of those recent Sundays when she'd sneaked into the back of the church after the service had started, and sneaked out before she'd had to face folks.

He'd talked about hating the sin and forgiving the sinner. A daunting task, she'd thought at the time.

Had she been on the pastor's mind when he prepared that sermon? She wouldn't put it past him.

She sat down on the steps and wrapped her arms around her knees, recalling Jesus' words in Matthew, chapter 5: *"Love your enemies, bless them that curse you, do good to them that hate you, and pray for them which despitefully use you, and persecute you."*

A tall order! But if she was going to heal, now was the time to begin.

She rested her cheek against her knees and stole a glance heavenward. "All right, Father, take my hate away. And—this is so hard. I—I want You to bless Kane. Bless him by showing Yourself to him."

That was the best she could do.

Yet, somehow, just saying the words, by asking His help, the suffocating weight that had been pressing her heart seemed to ease.

It hadn't been as difficult as she'd expected.

How hard she'd fought giving up what had separated her from everything she believed in and everyone she loved.

Which brought her to Isaac.

He had been intruding more and more into her thoughts, in a most disturbing way.

Ever since she could remember, the mosaic of her life had included Isaac. Through good times and bad, his devotion, his loyalty, his faithfulness, had been unshakable. The bond between them had grown deeper than friendship. It was built on a foundation of shared experiences, understanding, humor, and a depth of feeling strong enough to endure life's most bitter assaults.

A verse from Proverbs came to mind: *"Length of days, and long life, and peace, shall they add to thee. Let not mercy and truth forsake thee: bind them about thy neck; write them upon the table of thine heart."*

These words expressed exactly how she felt about Isaac. He was always with her, "written on the table of her heart."

What was love anyway, but that?

She'd gotten it all wrong. She'd been seduced by honeyed words, smoldering glances, stolen kisses.

All this time, she'd been searching for her one true love, and he had been standing right there in front of her.

Abruptly, she rose. Tomorrow, she would make things right!

In her mind she saw his dear face, his warm, loving eyes. She smiled, remembering the moment when he'd grabbed her so impetuously on the worship center's steps.

He wasn't all that bad a kisser, either!

❧

"Morning, Spike," she sang out, pushing through her office door the next day.

Spike came out of the back room carrying a pail and mop. "Isaac stopped to say good-bye."

"Good-bye?" Jane frowned.

"Said he's sorry to have missed you. That he'd be in touch." Spike slapped the wet mop onto the floor and began swishing it around.

"Did he say where he was going?"

"Didn't say."

"Did he say how long he'd be gone?"

"Nope. But I got the feeling it would be for a spell, or he wouldn't have bothered to stop by."

Her heart sank. "You're sure he didn't say how long?"

"You might ask Zeke. He drove him to the station."

"He went by train?"

"Uh-huh." Spike disappeared down the hall.

Jane stared at the empty doorway.

Concern locked itself around her heart. It wasn't like Isaac to just go away like that, not without making a point of telling her first.

But why should he? The way she'd been avoiding him.

A man could be expected to put up with just so much.

Maybe he'd reached his limit.

No, she couldn't believe that. She wouldn't believe it! Even so, she still couldn't bring herself to go ask Jackie Lee when—if—he was returning.

Two days later, when she heard a knock and pulled open the front door to find Isaac standing there, she sagged with relief.

He stood on her porch, holding a fishing rod, a bunch of wildflowers tucked into the blue bow tied around its top. "Brought you a birthday present."

He was present enough, she was so glad to see his sweet freckled face. "It's not my birthday."

"I missed your last four. Remember?"

How could she forget? She looked up at him, so big and strong and comforting. Dear Isaac.

Who knew better than Isaac how to make her laugh when she felt like crying; who sensed when her heart was breaking and how to mend it? She realized he'd been waiting to do just that. Mend her heart.

She held up her hands. "I have something important to tell you and it isn't easy, so please don't interrupt me. I'm—I'm not heartbroken!"

Isaac looked as shocked as she was by the sudden admission.

And then the words spewed out, tumbling over each other in a breathless stream. "I'm humiliated and I'm angry. I'm angry at that scoundrel and what he almost did to our little town. And I'm angry at myself for the part I had in it, and I'm angry for not seeing through him and being blind and naive and not trusting what you tried to tell me; and for being taken in by his false charm and sweet talk, and—but. . .I'm not heartbroken, and that's the truth of it. Why. . . Why, I've hardly been thinking about him at all." She gulped. "I've been thinking about you," she blurted out.

Isaac took a deep breath and let it out slowly.

Jane waited, staring down at the ground, her heart pounding. And waited and waited. Finally, she stamped her foot and cried out, "Isaac August, don't just stand there. Aren't you going to say anything?"

"Wanna go fishin'?"

Just like old times. She couldn't suppress a giggle. "That sounds like a romantic invitation."

"It could be." He grinned. "Grab your shawl."

She barely managed to throw it over the shoulders of her blue frock before he pulled her out the door and shut it behind her, drawing her down a path carpeted with the colorful leaves of autumn.

Suddenly she stopped. "Where did you get that?" She pointed out toward the road.

"It's mine?"

"You can't afford a fancy buggy like that."

"I can now. Billy Murray is going to record one of my songs for the Lambert Company."

"Why, he's a famous singer." Jane clapped her hands. "Isaac, why didn't you tell me? Oh, that was a silly question, wasn't it?" She gazed back, abashed. "Is that why you've been gone the past two days, to buy this. . .sporty two-seater?"

"I wanted to surprise you."

"Well, you certainly succeeded." She smiled up at him, suddenly shy.

And after all she'd put him through.

He looked down at her, returning her smile with such warmth it spilled into her very soul.

Suddenly he turned and, tossing the fishing rod behind the maroon leather seat, he helped her up. "The Lambert Company produces discs and cylinders for the Victor Talking Machine Company. They want me to come to New York to discuss publishing a whole songbook. In fact, they gave me quite an advance. I guess they think folks are gonna like my little ditties," he said modestly.

"Oh, my goodness. You'll be famous," she cried as he jogged around and hopped in next to her.

"I don't know about that." He picked up the reins.

"It's everything you ever dreamed." She stopped, an awful thought suddenly occurring to her. "Does that mean you'll be leaving Whispering Bluff?" she whispered.

He pulled the pony to a halt. "Would you miss me, Janie?" he murmured, his gaze averted.

"What do you think?"

He dropped the reins and faced her, flinging his arm over the back of the seat. "Why don't you come with me?"

Jane's mouth dropped open. Her heart plummeted. "Why, Isaac August, I can't believe you'd even suggest such a scandalous thing."

Isaac began to laugh. "This isn't a proposition, Jane, it's a proposal."

"A proposal? Oh." She dropped her gaze, chagrined that she'd contemplated, for even an instant, dishonorable intentions. "This is—this is awfully sudden, Isaac," she murmured.

"You think so?" He touched her sleeve. "How about seventeen years? Since that day you gave me a bloody nose in second grade. I knew right then you were in love with me."

"That was an accident."

"So you claim." He played with the fringe on her ecru shawl. "Well, what do you say, Janie?"

"If I were to say yes," she said slowly, "would we be coming back to Whispering Bluff?"

He grinned. "I have to come back. Who'd take care of my fine buggy? Besides, you have your career."

"You can't always count on a second term in this profession." She giggled. "Spike might have political aspirations, you know." She thought for a moment. "Where will we live? I love my little cottage," she said wistfully, "but it's a bit small for a family."

Isaac's voice was husky. "That sounds like a yes."

"I guess it is." She gazed up at him. "You knew the exact moment that I realized how much I love you. You really are my soul mate."

"Oh, Janie."

She looked down again at her hands, clasped in her lap. "I guess I'm getting a little ahead of myself, talking about houses when we're not even formally engaged."

"Not at all," he said with the smug expression of a man who had thought of everything.

He reached into his jacket pocket and pulled out some folded sheets of paper, handing them to her.

Jane smoothed them out on her lap.

She stared over at him. "These are purchase and sale papers on Old Man Craig's place."

"Yep!"

"You were pretty confident!"

"Not confident, Janie. Hopeful. I haven't signed 'em yet." His serious expression turned teasing. " 'Course, my first choice would have been Ludd's ranch, but he wasn't sellin' and I'm not that rich." He tweaked her nose and gave her a poke.

Then he drew her into his arms.

And he kissed her. And he kissed her and he kissed her, with passionate kisses the way only a man who had been waiting most of his life could kiss.

And she returned them as only a woman could, who had, at last, found the right home for her seeking heart.

A Letter To Our Readers

Dear Reader:
In order that we might better contribute to your reading enjoyment, we would appreciate your taking a few minutes to respond to the following questions. We welcome your comments and read each form and letter we receive. When completed, please return to the following:

Fiction Editor
Heartsong Presents
PO Box 719
Uhrichsville, Ohio 44683

1. Did you enjoy reading *Out of the Ashes* by Rachel Druten?
   ❏ Very much! I would like to see more books by this author!
   ❏ Moderately. I would have enjoyed it more if

   _____

   _____

   _____

2. Are you a member of **Heartsong Presents**? ❏ Yes ❏ No
   If no, where did you purchase this book? _____

   _____

3. How would you rate, on a scale from 1 (poor) to 5 (superior), the cover design? _____

4. On a scale from 1 (poor) to 10 (superior), please rate the following elements.

   ____ Heroine   ____ Plot
   ____ Hero   ____ Inspirational theme
   ____ Setting   ____ Secondary characters

5. These characters were special because? _____

_____

_____

6. How has this book inspired your life? _____

_____

_____

7. What settings would you like to see covered in future **Heartsong Presents** books? _____

_____

_____

8. What are some inspirational themes you would like to see treated in future books? _____

_____

_____

9. Would you be interested in reading other **Heartsong Presents** titles? ❑ Yes ❑ No

10. Please check your age range:

    ❑ Under 18   ❑ 18-24

    ❑ 25-34   ❑ 35-45

    ❑ 46-55   ❑ Over 55

Name _____

Occupation _____

Address _____

City, State, Zip _____